Jamaica Bay

Bill Perks

Publications Ltd

PUBLISHED BY PLOD PUBLICATIONS LTD

Copyright © Bill Perks 2006

ISBN-13 978-0-9552932-0-7 (hardback)
ISBN-10 0-9552932-0-0 (hardback)
ISBN-13 978-0-9552932-1-4 (paperback)
ISBN-10 0-9552932-1-9 (paperback)

A catalogue record for this title is available from the British Library

Set by Plod Publications Ltd, 26a Richmond Road, Olton, Solihull, West Midlands, UK, B92 7RP
Printed and bound in the United Kingdom by TJ International, Padstow, Cornwall

For further information on Plod Publications Ltd, visit our website at:
www.plodpublications.co.uk

To Ian and Jo … rare magic indeed

Chapter 1

Jim sat on the arm of his dad's favourite chair in the living room with his elbows leaning on the window ledge, staring aimlessly through the window into Shelly Street. The smooth tarmac shone in the rain and made Jim think of brighter days when he might go fishing with his dad.

It was only the second week of his summer holidays, and already he was bored with nothing to do. He had sat in his present position, near the window, for what seemed like hours. His mum's net curtain was draped over the back of his head, and Jim's face was so close to the cold glass that all around him a thick misty fog stuck to the window like soggy paper.

There was nothing to see in the street outside; very few cars came along and nobody with any sense would walk anywhere in this weather. Jim stared at a small bird investigating the contents of the bird-table in the middle of the small patch of grass in front of his house. There was no prospect of anything interesting happening.

'Jim?' came a voice from the kitchen. 'Jim?'

Jim thought that he ought to answer his mum, but he really couldn't raise the energy to call back.

'James, where are you?' her voice was getting louder.

'I'm in the front room,' Jim called back.

His mother came into the room wiping her hands on her apron. She always wore an apron over her clothes when she was indoors and she always seemed to be busy doing things. Jim often thought that even when the house looked really tidy his mum always found things to do — and she often found things for Jim to do, much to his annoyance.

'Why are you moping around in here? There must be some things you'd like to play with upstairs.'

'James, I'm talking to you. Don't be rude.'

Jim recognised the warning in her voice 'I'm sorry, Mum, but I'm so fed up. I know I've got things upstairs but there's nothing I want to play with. If I had a mouse to look after I'd be okay.'

'Oh here we go again!' shouted his mum, 'How many times must you be told? You are not having a mouse.' She moved a couple of small ornaments on the mantelpiece, impatiently checking for dust.

Jim had tried to introduce the subject of having a mouse several times before, but his mum refused point blank to allow it.

'But Simon's got one, Mum.'

'Simon's mum and dad must be mad to allow it. They are dirty little creatures and I will not have them in the house,' she said with finality. Jim knew when to keep quiet.

Simon was the boy who used to live next door at number 40. His birthday was the week before Jim's and they had been best friends ever since Jim could remember. Simon and his family had moved away during the summer half-term holiday in June. His dad worked for a firm making furniture. When it shut down, he had been given the choice of moving to Scotland to work, and so they had gone.

Jim and Simon thought it really was unfair to split up their friendship but it happened all the same. Maybe that was why Jim was fed up.

'Well, I'm not having you being miserable all day under my feet,' Mum said, 'If you don't find yourself something to do then I will have no problem finding you something useful to help me with.'

When Jim's mother put it to him like that he realised he had no choice but to go upstairs and discover some time-filling occupation. As if to reinforce what Jim had been thinking earlier, his mother ushered him away from the window, drew back the net curtain and began vigorously cleaning the foggy glass with a cloth she had concealed in her apron.

She then stood back examining her work as if she were reading a notice. Apparently satisfied, she replaced the curtain and started humming as she left the front room to return to the kitchen. She always hummed when she was happy with life.

'We're having beans on toast for lunch,' she called, as if trying to create some excitement. As he clumped slowly up the stairs, Jim put his mind to what he could do up until lunch time, and then after lunch, and then tomorrow and the next day and the next. He lay on the bed and stared at the ceiling. He smiled to himself as he looked at the little luminous stars and dots that lit up his bedroom at night and glowed as if they were alive. He felt comforted by them.

It was then he remembered a book under his wardrobe. He fetched it out and sat on his bed with a look of longing in his eyes. The book was an old holiday brochure showing some very sunny pictures of beaches and rolling hills of beautiful England.

Jim's mum and dad did not explain why, but many weeks ago they had said it would be impossible to have a family holiday that summer. Jim never asked why. It was just the thought of spending six and a half weeks at home with nothing to do and, now that Simon was gone, not even a friend to play with.

'What on earth am I going to do?' he thought.

At six o'clock that evening Jim went downstairs and took his usual place at the tea table. His parents were already seated. His dad, Mike, worked in the wages office at a local biscuit factory, and he still had his shirt and tie on as he sat opposite Jim, with a concerned look on his face.

Taking another look at his mum, Jim noticed she had an unusual expression on her gentle face as well. He wondered why.

'Eat your tea dear,' she said.

The meal continued in silence. Still a strange look played on the faces of his parents between chewing.

His curiosity finally got the better of him.

'Dad, is something wrong?' Jim asked.

'Oh go on, Mike. Tell him,' cried his mother.

'Tell me what?' said Jim.

His dad put down his knife and fork, and wiped the corners of his mouth with his napkin. He took hold of his wife's hand and looked at Jim.

'Now young James, what I am about to tell you is nothing to concern yourself about so don't worry.'

Jim started to worry.

'We said to you that it would not be possible to have a family holiday this year. The reason for that is, unfortunately, your mum has to go into hospital for a time. It's not life threatening or anything like that so don't worry. It's just that when she comes out of hospital she will need a long time to rest and get better.'

'I'll look after you, Mum. Don't you worry about that. You can tell me what to do and I'll do it and look after you and scrub the floors and . . .'

'James, hang on, hang on,' said his dad. 'With your mum in hospital and me at work it means we are going to have to find somewhere for you to stay for a couple of weeks.'

Jim sat back as if he'd been hit by his dad. Where on earth could his parents send him, out of the way, from under their feet? Then he had a brilliant idea.

'Perhaps I could go and stay with Simon's family!' he said hopefully.

'We thought of that,' said his mum.

'Simon's mum is having another baby, and they don't think they could cope with a visitor for a long period of time.'

Jim looked from his mum to his dad and back again. It seemed obvious there was something they hadn't told him. They had already decided where he was going.

His mum confirmed this. 'Do you remember me talking to you about your Great Uncle Tom, my dad's brother?'

Before Jim had a chance to say that he had no recollection of him, his dad went on. 'Yes, you remember — after the Second World War he went to live in the West Indies. Well a few months ago he moved back to England to a place near the sea in Cornwall. He says he'd love to see you and, if you would like to, you can stay there for a while, just until Mum is better.'

There was a long pause. 'And what if I don't want to?' asked Jim.

'Well there isn't anywhere else, Jim darling. I'll get better as quickly as I can and you can come home. Uncle Tom really is nice. I think you'll get on very well.'

His mum's voice was pleading. She was getting upset, her eyes filling with tears.

It was then that Jim decided to show how grown up he could be and smiled as much as he could. 'I don't mind, Mum. If it means you getting better I'll go, but when will I have to go?'

Mr Wills drew himself up to his full height whilst sitting down and, having pulled in a big breath as if to exert his full authority, he said, 'Saturday, the day after tomorrow.'

Chapter 2

The next day seemed to shoot by. Jim's mum didn't have too much to say except for things like 'Your dad will miss you so much,' and 'You'll really like your Uncle Tom.'

If Jim was told to put his favourite toys in a bag once, he was told at least a dozen times. All he could think about was what his Great Uncle Tom would really be like. What parents say about someone or something can be totally different from how it actually is.

Jim continually badgered his mum with questions like; 'How old is he?', 'When was the last time you saw Uncle Tom?', 'Is Uncle Tom married?', 'Has he ever met me before?'

No matter what question he asked his mum, the reply was always something like; 'There's no need to worry' or 'You'll be able to ask Uncle Tom all these things yourself.'

Jim noticed a bit of a change in his mum. She didn't hum the whole day; she even seemed a bit miserable. Eventually Jim forgot his own problems and realised that she was probably worried about her visit to hospital. He had found out it was an operation that quite a lot of ladies have to have. He thought he would leave it at that, as he didn't like to think about operations and blood and the funny clean smell that most doctors' surgeries seemed to have.

At the end of the day three large bags had been packed. There was a large white envelope pinned to the largest bag saying 'UNCLE TOM' in big capital letters. Jim wasn't told what it contained.

He went to bed that night knowing that he wouldn't sleep much. The little stars and dots glowed on his ceiling, and if he stayed really quiet he imagined he could hear the distant noise of the sea breaking over long sandy beaches and the screech of gulls fishing for their supper. For the first time Jim realised he was going to the seaside after all — and, who knows, there might be a great deal of fun to be had.

The Wills family set off bright and early the next morning with Jim's whole world packed in the boot. The journey to Cornwall took most of the day, although Jim's dad drove so slowly it seemed to make the distance longer. You could not call him quick. This left Jim plenty of time to ponder what awaited him at his Uncle Tom's. He soon had a picture in his head of what Uncle Tom looked like. He thought he may be similar to his mum, not too big, normally quiet, probably a sensible looking man.

The further south they travelled, the better the weather seemed to get. It hadn't been raining when they left home but it certainly wasn't swimming costume time. Now the sun shone and there were fewer and fewer clouds in the sky. Spirits lifted and the Wills family even managed eleven verses of 'The cow kicked Nelly in the belly in the barn.'

It was gone tea time when the holiday resort of Newquay came and went. There seemed to be lots of happy people around smiling and sporting deep sun tans. Even though the car didn't stop, Jim could tell that Newquay felt like a place to have fun.

'It's only about ten miles from here I think,' said Dad.

All signs of civilisation were soon left behind and they travelled mile after mile of rugged country cliff roads with occasional glimpses of the glistening sea accompanied by the shriek of gulls playing in the warm air. With a right hand turn the road changed into a dirt track and sank into a wood.

Suddenly the engine stopped, and everyone sat in the car staring at the building which stood before them. It was obviously a house, but whether it was lived in or not was a different thing. It was at least three times bigger than 42 Shelly Street. The track finished and turned into a footpath which ran beside the house.

Surely nobody could live in a place like this. There were no bricks in evidence. The whole place seemed to be made of large planks of wood, some of which had been repaired again and again with pieces of timber of all colours and sizes.

A large veranda ran the whole length of the front of the house, and Jim immediately thought of television programmes he had seen about Americans living in the mountains of Virginia with big, big families.

For what seemed like ages nobody moved, until from the big front door came a loud grinding squeak, as it was opened inwards. Deep shadow masked any view of the person now occupying the doorway, but as if a special signal had been given, Jim and his parents got out of the car and gathered in front of it, feeling somewhat nervous.

'Hello, Uncle Tom,' said Mum.

She sounded very, very nervous, which really made Jim feel worse. If his mum and dad were afraid of Uncle Tom, then what chance did little James Wills stand?

Heavy footsteps sounded on the old floor boards as Uncle Tom came into the light for the first time. As one, Jim and his parents took a huge intake of breath as the full size of the man came into view.

He was gigantic, or at least he seemed to be. Admittedly he was two or three feet above them but he looked like a mountain. He wore huge brown boots that had all the leather knocked off the toes leaving shiny grey steel. The man's massive bulk seemed to be forced into a brown boiler suit which, although it looked clean, had obviously seen better days. Perched on his head was an old straw trilby-type hat which was losing its shape and some of its straw. What struck Jim more than anything was the face of Uncle Tom.

His head seemed much too big for his body which was probably due to the enormous bushy silver beard which trailed down his chest. His silvery hair stuck out from beneath his hat like pieces of grass. From beneath the shadow of the hat his deep blue eyes seemed to glow like beacons in the night. The other thing that struck Jim was that for the first time he understood what people meant when they talked about having crow's feet at the corner of their eyes.

These lines that Uncle Tom had were so deep they almost looked like make-up. Four lines. Four lines that told anyone that this man had lived a long and interesting life.

'Well don't just stand there making the place look untidy. Come in and have a cup of tea or something.' He had a very deep voice with the strangest accent that Jim had ever heard.

With those few words he turned round and went back indoors. The small family, still huddled together, looked at each other for a moment and then cautiously made their way up the steps and into the dingy light of the veranda.

Like a blanket the strange atmosphere reached out and swallowed Jim as his parents seemed to push him before them into the house. A long wide hallway led directly into a very spacious kitchen where Uncle Tom stood, legs astride with his hands behind his back. Jim shuffled forward until he was standing in front of the giant, with the big searchlight eyes boring down on him.

As everyone seemed to be waiting for Jim to do or say something, like an ancient ritual he did what he thought was the most appropriate thing to do — he thrust his arm out with his hand extended and said, 'It's very nice to meet you, sir.'

The room exploded with a thunderous noise, and at first Jim thought his uncle might burst with pain but then he realised Uncle Tom was roaring with laughter. He put his hands on his knees and he laughed and laughed. Jim took the opportunity to get a good look at his uncle's face and noticed that tears were dropping from his cheeks. Before he knew what was happening, his uncle, still roaring with laughter, had grabbed hold of his hips and thrust him into the air like a rocket.

'So you are James George Wills, my great nephew. Well you, young man, are most welcome to the hospitality that my simple home can offer.' And he continued laughing.

Putting Jim down gingerly he rushed over to Jean, his mum, and gave her a great big bear hug. It seemed to Jim that he was going to squeeze the very life out of her. Things had certainly taken a turn for the better, a turn that Jim had not expected. It was only at this point that Jim learnt just how much his mum and dad had kept him in the dark about this strange man who now stood before him, his Uncle Tom — and indeed how much planning had gone into his visit to Jamaica Bay.

Chapter 3

Uncle Tom made the tea for Jim and his parents who sat around the large scrubbed kitchen table which dominated the floor space. It seemed as though the whole house got brighter, the more relaxed Jim became. His great uncle's accent certainly was very strange; it was almost as if he sang his words. It was very interesting, listening to a brief life history of Uncle Tom — how he had been in the Merchant Navy during the war, spending a lot of his time off the Americas. It seemed a natural step, once hostilities had ceased, that he should settle down in a country that welcomed people with a knowledge of the outside world who were willing to help stabilise things. The reason for his return to Britain seemed a bit uncertain but it coincided with the death of his brother, Jim's granddad.

When the tea was finished Uncle Tom spoke to Jim's dad. 'Mike, why don't you go for a short walk to the cliffs while I show this young whippersnapper round my humble abode? If you follow the path out front you'll reach the cliff in about 200 metres.' As he spoke the big man pointed towards the front door.

'Okay,' said Jim's dad. 'You be good,' he said, directing a heavy frown at Jim.

As Mr and Mrs Wills went outside, Jim followed his great uncle into the hallway and up the stairs which faced the front door.

'I hope you don't mind, Jim, but I thought you could sling your hook in the attic. I've had it cleaned up, and it's a really big room; probably very cold in the winter, but just right in the summer.' They reached the first floor landing and the old man turned around and looked at the small boy. 'What do you think then, Shrimp?' he asked.

'Sling your hook?' enquired Jim. 'Doesn't that mean "get out"?'

Once more there was the rumble and thunder of laughter as if it had started in those large brown boots and sprung out of his fuzzy beard like a volcano. 'Ha, ha, bless you, Jim. I'm an old sea dog and some habits die hard you know. I'll show you what I mean.'

Again Uncle Tom turned and climbed the stairs until they reached a door that took up the whole width of the staircase. They both stood motionless. Silence invaded Jim's mind. He was sucking in air as if he'd run a hundred metres, but the old man's breathing was slow and steady. Very deliberately Uncle Tom turned the wooden handle and gently pushed the door open.

Sunlight flooded the stairs and made Jim put his arm up to protect his eyes from the glare. The room was very big with a chest of drawers and two tall wardrobes lined up neatly behind the door. The sloping roof was very lofty in the middle, leaving the walls about 6 feet high. At each end of the room was a large window through which a fresh-smelling breeze blew. Faded rugs covered the floor leaving large gaps here and there showing the old stained floorboards.

'You'll have to go downstairs for the toilet and a wash and things like that Jim, but I think you'll be all right up here. Look out of the window and tell me what you can see.'

He rushed to the window, which came up to his middle, and leaned out slightly. The treetops seemed to drop away from the house, and above them Jim saw the most wonderful sight he could ever imagine. A million lights sparkled in the sea where the sun shone and reflected like tiny mirrors. The ocean went on for ever, and further round to the right he could just make out the craggy face of a cliff which looked as old as time itself. Like little ants walking above the cliff he could see the white cardigan and blue shirt of his mum and dad. He shouted and waved his arms but they were too far away to notice him. He felt a huge paw on each shoulder and the warmth of his great uncle as he stood behind him.

'I think things are going to be okay, Uncle Tom,' said Jim.

'I'm sure they are, Jim. Cast your eyes over here my lad, and I'll show you where your hook is.'

Old habits certainly did die hard with the old sailor. He was holding what looked like the end of a huge string bag, which was attached to the wall by a large steel ring on a hook. Uncle Tom stretched the string bag and holding another steel ring on the opposite end, looped it over another large hook that was situated in the wall near the window. The two walls and the string bag formed a triangle. To Jim's amazement his Uncle took hold of the middle of the string bag and holding it behind him, he thrust himself backwards throwing himself full length. If Uncle Tom's boiler suit had been green he would have reminded Jim of a pea pod, for there he lay swinging from side to side with the edges of his string platform curled around him, and his big hands joined behind his head. Now Jim understood. The one thing missing from his room was a bed, and the full realisation had just struck home — that this was where Uncle Tom expected him to sleep during his stay.

'You try, Jim,' said Uncle Tom, not being very successful at keeping the humour from his voice, as he lightly sprang from his position. There was an old packing case in the corner of the room, which the old man picked up and put under the string bag.

'I've slept in a hammock for over fifty years now Jim and I don't think I could manage in a bed any more. It may seem difficult at first but take it from me young fella, you'll be jumping in and out of there like a herring in a pot before you can say "barnacles".'

Jim stepped on to the box and opened the hammock whilst trying to place his right knee in its centre. As soon as he put his weight onto his knee he fell headlong with a yelp into a big heap against the wall. Huge gasps of laughter rang around the room as once again Uncle Tom doubled up with his hands on his knees, and rocked from side to side. The sight was so funny, Jim joined in and for what seemed like ages the two laughed together, at each other. Eventually Jim got up and with the steadying influence of the old sailor, he managed to climb into the hammock and was left suspended in the air, swinging from side to side.

'You have a look around, Jim. I've got some chicken and rice in the oven that needs looking at. Come down when you are ready for tea.'

'Uncle Tom?' said Jim hesitantly.

'Yes.' It sounded like he was expecting some awful revelation from the small boy.

'Thanks for saying you'll look after me. I'll try not to be too much trouble.'

The old man came back into the room, and went up to Jim's side. His eyes sparkled as he said, 'Jamaica Bay is your home for the foreseeable future and you are to treat it so. The most important thing is that your mum gets better double quick. In the meantime we'll have bucket loads of fun, right?' Chuckling to himself, he turned and went downstairs whistling some unrecognisable tune.

'Jamaica Bay, what a lovely name for this house,' Jim thought, 'How it conjures up a warm feeling inside when you say it – Jamaica Bay.'

He lay there for a little while pondering his immediate future, and then he realised he couldn't get out of the hammock without help, which at this time was two floors below him.

'Things are going to be okay,' he said to himself. 'You just wait and see.'

Half an hour later Mike and Jean Wills were seated at the kitchen table with the heady aroma of spicy chicken and pineapple juice filling the air.

'Where's Jim got to Uncle Tom?' asked the concerned mother.

'He's still looking round his room,' smiled the old man.

At that moment a loud yell and a heavy thud were heard from upstairs.

'Oh, Jim!' cried his mum.

Uncle Tom laughed. 'He's managed to get out of his hammock at last.' The thought amused him greatly. 'He'll be okay.'

Footsteps were heard down the stairs and moments later a very red-faced Jim appeared, hiding a tight grimace.

'There, I told you so,' said Uncle Tom as he turned to welcome Jim.

'Are you all right?' asked his mum.

'Yes, it's okay. I was just getting used to sleeping in a hammock. You ought to see it, Dad! You can see the sea from my window and I even saw you and Mum walking on the cliff. You can see right over the trees and everything and ...'

'It sounds to me as though you are going to have a good time stopping with your Great Uncle Tom,' said his dad.

'It'll be all right,' said Jim in a non-committal sort of voice.

'Sit down, Shrimp, and experience some real Caribbean cooking,' said the old man, with a satisfied expression on his face.

Jim didn't know what to expect from the large ovenproof dish that was put in the middle of the table. It certainly smelt good and he wasn't really surprised to learn that it tasted even better. With a rich sweet lumpy sauce, that Uncle Tom insisted was mango chutney, and sweaty rice, the spicy chicken was absolutely delicious. Jim wiped his plate clean with a piece of bread roll and downed his glass of pineapple juice. Jim's parents did not altogether miss the fact that Uncle Tom did exactly the same as their son with his bread roll but they decided to act in a slightly more refined manner leaving their knives and forks pulled together on top of their empty plates.

'Well,' said Uncle Tom. 'What do you think to my cooking?'

'It was certainly different,' commented Mr Wills somewhat uncertainly, 'but I think I enjoyed it.'

'It was fantastic, Uncle Tom! The most delicious chicken I have ever tasted,' said Jim.

'Good. Does anyone want ice-cream?' asked Uncle Tom. Everyone declined, much to his obvious disappointment.

'It really is time we were going,' said Jim's dad. 'It'll be the wee small hours before we get home as it is.'

Once again Jim's mind was forced to think about his mum's problems. All his cases and bags were taken upstairs to the attic, where he proudly showed off his new bed.

'Are you sure he will be all right in that thing?' Jim's mum asked the old man.

'Yes of course he will. Stop fussing, girl. It will be good for the boy.'

Once back downstairs, Jim gave his dad a hug and then rather tearfully said good-bye to his mum. Quite wisely they didn't hang about long and left quickly, disappearing in a cloud of dust up the narrow track that would once again take them back to civilisation. Jim found himself waving even though the car had vanished from view. He could still hear it, but it soon faded and he suddenly felt quite alone. He turned around and saw his Great Uncle Tom sitting on a large chair that was fixed onto a cradle-type frame, which allowed the chair to swing slowly backwards and forwards.

He hadn't noticed it before. The old man had a very long white clay pipe in his mouth, which he seemed to be content with sucking gently and allowing the sweet smelling smoke to drift away in the night. He patted the seat next to him gesturing to Jim to sit down. They sat for a long time without saying anything as the sun got lower in the sky and dusk fell on Jamaica Bay.

Apparently sensing Jim's mood, Uncle Tom said very slowly, 'I know you are feeling a little bit funny inside right now, Jim boy, but your mum will be okay and I will look after you. You can always come to me with your problems you know. I will always be here for you.'

This made Jim feel a whole lot better. He gently leant against his great uncle who put a massive arm round him and gave a small squeeze.

'Well now, whilst at Jamaica Bay I'm afraid everything is shared, even the washing up, so — jump about let's get going. I don't want Maureen finding a great mess now you've turned up when she gets here in the morning.'

'Who's Maureen?' shouted Jim as his uncle disappeared into the house.

'Ah ha, you'll see,' came the reply. 'Wait till the morning.'

With the washing up done a wave of tiredness swept over the young boy, after the tension and excitement of the day. He visited the massive bathroom on the first floor, and then went to his room in the attic. Here he found his uncle fiddling with the troublesome hammock.

'There, Jim. I've put a cord over to the wall to steady it a bit for getting in and out. Once you're in you can take it off that small hook.' He had also put a layer of soft mattress on the string to make it more comfortable.

'Sleep well, young Jim, and I will see you in the morning. Okay?'

'Good night Uncle Tom, and thanks.'

The door closed and far from being a bit afraid, Jim felt as if he was somehow meant to stay in this house. It felt warm and cosy and as he rocked gently in the hammock he looked out of the window, and once again saw the stars and dots glowing like friendly flies, but this time the ceiling was much much higher and the stars were real. He felt the warm breeze from the open window, and he gave a big contented smile. Then he slept a long comfortable sleep, rocking slowly from side to side.

Chapter 4

Jim woke with a start, and at first he didn't have a clue where he was. The bright sunshine flooded through the window, and then he remembered the events of the previous day. Gathering his thoughts quickly, he tried to clamber out of his hammock, but only succeeded in making it rock violently to and fro. Then he remembered the cord his great uncle had fixed to the hammock to steady it. He would soon get the hang of it. Meanwhile Uncle Tom stood at the kitchen sink talking to a woman who sat at the table drinking a mug of hot tea.

'Yes he's certainly had a good night's sleep, considering he is a stranger here,' said the old man. 'I went up three times last night and he had a big grin on his face the whole time.'

'How you can make him sleep on that contraption I'll never know. It must be so difficult for him,' said the woman.

Just then a loud yelp followed by a heavy thud echoed down the stairs. The big man rocked silently with laughter. 'There you see — he's awake at last, and by the sounds of things getting to grips with his sleeping tackle.'

A few minutes later Jim came down the stairs into the kitchen. His fair hair was sticking up at right angles to his head, and his rosy cheeks bore the marks of having been threatened with a flannel and water. The woman at the table got up and stretched her hand out to Jim.

'Hello, Jim. My name is Maureen. I come in most days and help your uncle keep this place in some sort of order.'

'It's nice to meet you,' said Jim. 'How far away do you live?'

Maureen had a very nice friendly face, one that you could imagine being attached to a nurse. Her black hair showed the odd grey tinge here and there, but Jim imagined her to be quite young, about his mum's age.

'Me and Gemma live just down the path towards the cliff. The path stretches right to the next village, and there are the odd lunatics like me and your uncle who like to live in these remote places,' replied Maureen.

'Who's Gemma?' enquired Jim.

'You'll meet her in a minute,' said Maureen. 'She's my daughter. In the holidays she comes with me to help Tom — I mean "Uncle" Tom.'

At that moment the door at the back of the kitchen opened, and a young girl with a tanned face came in.

'I've got six today, Uncle Tom,' she cried. 'Oh hello. You must be Jim. My name is Gemma.'

They stood looking at each other, each one weighing the other up. Like her mother, she had black hair which was cut almost as short as Jim's. She had several big freckles on her nose and great big brown eyes.

'Well, six eggs Gemma, that's not too bad. Looks like they've picked up their laying just in time for Jim's visit,' said Uncle Tom.

Sensing the slight tension between Gemma and Jim he went on. 'Sit down you two young 'uns and let's get some breakfast down you.'

Jim sat down but Gemma turned round, putting the basket on one of the worktops and said, 'Thanks, but I'm not hungry.' With that, she went back outside.

'Don't worry about her, Jim,' said Maureen, 'She's not used to having someone her own age around. She'll get used to you, you'll see.'

"You'll see." When you are young, it is amazing how many times "You'll see" is said to you.

When breakfast was finished Jim was fully prepared to wipe up, but Maureen ushered both Jim and his great uncle away, and told them she was sure they had lots to do. So Uncle Tom showed Jim right round the whole house, starting with two rooms at the front.

One was a library-cum-study. Jim wasn't sure what his great uncle had to study, but the room had a cosy atmosphere, apart from the smell of damp books — or was it mildewed leather? It was very musty anyway. His uncle gave Jim permission to use his desk whenever he liked, to write home to his mum and dad or to his friends. Friends, thought Jim. He couldn't think of anyone he wished to write to.

The other room was filled with comfortable chairs, probably ten or more. There were leather ones and some prickly-looking material-covered ones; there were even some very large round wicker-type ones. This room was very quiet. Through an open doorway, Jim could see a conservatory. This was a lot smaller, with four of the large round wicker chairs and a coffee table.

'The room above this is my pride and joy,' said Uncle Tom. 'It's my special room. You'll see,' he said.

Suddenly, as if by magic, Jim could see a look in his uncle's eyes that transformed his face to look like a young man's again. The room he was referring to must be something really special to Uncle Tom. It made Jim feel like a conspirator to be let in on a very secret idea or plan. Upstairs he was shown three large bedrooms all pretty much the same size with the usual furniture in. The rooms, although tidy, looked as if they hadn't been decorated for years. One of the rooms was decorated in ancient steam engines rushing to their destination.

The last bedroom was obviously occupied by his uncle. It was quite sparsely furnished, with a large hammock fitted to the wall in one corner. In another corner was a door that his uncle stepped up to. Then taking a key from his trouser pocket he unlocked the door and pushed it open. Jim took a deep breath as he stared round the room. He was impressed.

Like the conservatory downstairs, this room was covered on three sides by large windows. The view from there was almost as good as from Jim's room. In the middle stood a large ship's wheel measuring about five feet across its middle, with large spokes like those of a wagon wheel. He saw it was secured by a large rope that was lashed around the end of one of the spokes, and then onto the pillar that supported the roof almost in the middle of the room. There were tables with charts spread over them showing different Caribbean islands and some local coastline. Each chart was like a map of the sea with different depths marked and things to look out for like wrecks and sandbars. There were other instruments bolted in various positions around the benches, instruments that Jim didn't understand. When he looked around at his uncle the change was miraculous. With an old captain's hat on, he looked proud and every part the old sailor.

'Whenever I feel unhappy with life or when things are getting me down, I come up here and lose myself. I devoted some of my best years to the sea and all its hazards. No man can take away what I've had, Jim.'

His eyes looked far away as if he was reliving some memorable experience from long ago.

'What's this, Uncle Tom?' asked Jim, touching a long thick tube on a three-legged stand, which pointed out to sea.

The old man smiled and said, 'If you look out as far as you can to the horizon, Jim, do you see a small boat? It's very very tiny.'

'Yes,' replied Jim, squinting to try to deflect the glare.

Uncle Tom looked through the tube for a few moments and then, pulling an old milk crate over, he lifted Jim on to it and said, 'Shut one eye, Jim, and with the other look down the telescope.'

This the boy did dutifully.

'Now what do you see, boy?'

'Wow, that's really cool. It's a fishing boat. They're pulling something in on a rope.'

'That's right. If you look closely you will see some big black baskets being pulled in. If Frank is lucky, he'll be bringing some big lobsters to market at lunch time.'

'Do you know them then, Uncle Tom?' asked Jim.

'Sure I know them, boy. They work out of the next village. If you like I could ask them to take you out some day,' he suggested.

'No chance. No way. I'd be sea sick just stepping onto the boat, knowing me,' joked Jim.

'Well if you change your mind I'm sure it wouldn't be a problem. How about going to see Frank bring the boat in just after lunch, to see what he's caught?' suggested Uncle Tom.

'Yes, please,' replied Jim enthusiastically. 'I'd like that a lot.'

They spent a further few minutes chatting about the special room and its contents, and then Uncle Tom suggested they had a look around outside.

'Oh, before we do that I've got a little surprise for you, plus the last room which I completely forgot about because I never go down there.'

'Down there? Is it downstairs again? But we've seen all the rooms downstairs surely,' enquired Jim.

'Questions, questions, questions. I'm surprised you've got any room in there for any brains. Come on, Shrimp. I'll show you.'

'Don't tell me Uncle Tom,' said Jim. 'I'll see...'

They both laughed as they went downstairs, Uncle Tom once again in his straw hat.

Jim followed his uncle into the kitchen and through the door at the back into the yard.

Next to the back door was another door. Uncle Tom opened it, and stared into the darkness that seemed to seep out of the portal left where the door had been.

Gemma, who was sitting on an old log at the other side of the yard, called over. 'Where are you going, Uncle Tom?' she asked.

'Come with us,' he replied. 'We're only having a look in the cellar. You don't mind, do you, Jim?'

'No,' said Jim, thinking that if he had said yes, Gemma would have come anyway. Uncle Tom led the way down a very steep set of wooden steps that disappeared into a darkness so black it was blacker than black.

'You two wait there until I find a light.'

Uncle Tom disappeared as if walking into the mouth of a horrible monster. A dim light invaded the darkness at the foot of the steps and a voice called up.

'Okay, come on down you two.'

Gemma and Jim gave a brief glance at each other, and then gingerly tiptoed slowly down into the cellar. The room was half the size of the house itself, with a roof so low that Jim's uncle had to stoop to prevent his head banging on the large wooden rafters. The old sailor was fiddling with some ropes at the side of the room nearest the steps, and with a loud bang a wooden shutter opened like the giant cover of a book and fell flat on the ground outside, allowing sharp rays of light to infiltrate the dusty cavern. He did the same on two other walls with the same result and now the cellar was quite bright.

'It's the first time I've actually seen it with the shutters down,' said Uncle Tom, and as if to confirm this he began lifting various items off a large metal bench that ran the whole length of one wall, inspecting them like an old woman at a jumble sale. On what was obviously a cobbled floor, there lay a thick layer of coal dust and old straw with the occasional lump of debris from somebody's work at the bench. Wood and metal fragments were scattered over a large area and from the walls hung various old tools and chains.

It struck Jim how different from the rest of the house the cellar was. It was the only part he'd seen built mostly of stone. On the shutterless wall opposite the steps hung a very large chain, fixed through an anchorage ring set heavily into the wall. As he lifted it, the chain clanked with a dull low tone, which sounded almost sad.

'What's this chain for?' he asked.

'For hanging naughty boys from,' said Gemma with a giggle.

'I don't know,' said his Uncle. 'I assume it was for fixing something there, something quite large by the looks of the size of the chain.'

Just then, in the furthest corner of the cellar Jim spotted a shoebox. It stood out for some reason, but then almost immediately Jim knew why. It looked very clean and new, as if it had just been put there.

'What's that box, Uncle?' asked Jim.

'I don't know,' said Uncle Tom. 'You'd better have a look.'

Jim picked up the box. It was very light. He carefully lifted the lid off.

'It's only got straw in it!' he said with some disappointment. Then the straw moved and a tiny scratching sound came from inside. Jim carefully eased the layer of straw away, and there, sitting in a corner of the box, looking completely frightened, was a little white mouse. Its whiskers were twitching and its bright pink eyes looked up at him questioningly.

'Well, well, well,' said Uncle Tom in his strange accent. 'How on earth did that get here? Young Jim, looks like you'll have to look after it, don't you think?'

Jim looked up at the old man and saw his eyes twinkling. 'Thanks, Uncle Tom.'

'Well, when I was talking to your mum and dad about you coming to visit, I asked if there was anything you really wanted and your mum mentioned that you really wanted a mouse, so I thought I'd get you one.'

'He's great, thanks.' said Jim.

'Can I hold him?' asked Gemma.

'Of course you can,' replied Jim, 'as long as you're careful with him.'

Gemma picked the mouse up and let it run up her arm. She giggled as the little creature tickled her.

'Come on, Pinky,' said Jim. 'Let's take you upstairs to show Maureen.'

'Oh, I wouldn't do that if I were you,' said Gemma. 'Mum wouldn't be too pleased.'

'Leave him here for now,' said Uncle Tom. 'He's got some food, so he'll be quite safe. Pinky. Yes, I should have known you'd call him that.'

Jim put the box down again in the corner and the three of them made their way up the steps.

'You two can use the cellar as much as you like. I never use it, so call it your place, eh? Why don't you show Jim round the area Gemma, down to the cliffs? I'm sure he'd like to have a nose around. I need to sit down and have a cup of tea.'

So Gemma, apparently impressed now that Jim was a mouse owner, took him off into the wood to show him the best places to visit and to look at the sea, whilst Uncle Tom went back inside the house.

Jim was already having a great time at his new temporary home but he really wasn't expecting what Jamaica Bay had in store for him.

Chapter 5

For what seemed like hours, Gemma and Jim wandered slowly along the cliff tops, stopping occasionally for Gemma to point out various things, like the place where a ship was wrecked on the rocks 150 years ago, or the other wrecks before that.

'How come so many ships used to get smashed up here?' asked Jim.

'I don't really know,' said Gemma. 'Uncle Tom did tell me it was something to do with pirates showing lights where they shouldn't have done, making a ship believe there were dangers where there weren't and sending the doomed vessel onto the rocks. Then they would steal all the cargo and make a lot of money.'

Jim didn't really understand, but he kept quiet in case Gemma thought he was stupid and tried to tell him again. Talk of pirates and sunken treasure really was exciting, and the young boy from Shelly Street could not take everything in. It was like a dream world, he thought, just as if he had been transported to that old holiday brochure under his wardrobe at home. The pictures could well have been taken from where he stood now.

Jim leaned over the cliff edge as far as he dared to try and see to the very bottom, but the cliff was such a funny shape with so many enormous pieces sticking out, it was impossible to do.

Suddenly a piercing whistle broke the air, coming from the direction of the house, which Jim noticed for the first time rose from the trees like a floating island.

'What's that?' Jim whispered to Gemma.

'Oh, don't worry, Jim. That's just your uncle's way of saying, "come back".'

Gemma immediately broke into a trot and headed for the big old house, closely followed by her new friend. When the two children reached the house, they found Uncle Tom at the wheel of an old green Land Rover, with a canvas tent covering the back. Huge clouds of blue smoke filled the air, and the engine chugged throatily, giving the impression that there was no way it would move another yard.

'Jump in, you two. We'll go down to the quay to see what Frank's brought home,' shouted Uncle Tom above the engine noise.

The few miles to Pentilrock, the nearest village, seemed to take an eternity and the journey was made worse by the fact that a dense covering of blue smog was left behind as the old vehicle made steady progress. Other cars and vans blew their horns and drivers shook their fists whenever a straight piece of road allowed them to pass. This seemed to amuse Uncle Tom as he spent a lot of the journey rocking gently in his seat, his face creased in a smile. Conversation was impossible owing to on-board noise, but Jim noticed his uncle tapping his hand on the steering wheel, as if listening to a lively tune on the old radio, which looked incapable of making any sound at all.

Eventually Uncle Tom turned off the road, and headed through the busy little village until they reached a very untidy looking quayside. It was obviously the thing to do because quite a lot of people had formed into a group as a rusty fishing boat approached the only space left at the dock's edge. Jim guessed that many of the onlookers were holiday makers because of the noises some of them were making, 'OOOing' and 'ahhhing' as ropes were thrown from the boat to waiting men who quickly wrapped the thick snakes round huge concrete bollards positioned above the water's edge.

'Ahoy there, Frank! Permission to come aboard with two friends?' shouted Uncle Tom.

'Tom, nice to see you. If you don't mind laying off until we're ship-shape you are most welcome,' replied the man obviously in charge of the vessel. The name, Cornish Pride, was emblazoned on its bows. After a couple of minutes, following a sign from Frank, all three visitors scampered across the plank of wood that had been thrown between the boat and dry land. Jim felt like a visiting dignitary as he saw people in the crowd giving him envious looks.

The heady aroma of fish mixed with diesel fuel filled the air causing the children's nostrils to flare, but it wasn't a nasty smell, it seemed to fit in with being near the seaside, somehow comforting.

The four men who worked the boat fussed around frantically in an apparently disorganised mass, but it wasn't until Jim watched just one of them closely that he realised each of them had his own job to do and that together the team worked as one. There were big barrels of various colours, which contained some very strange looking creatures. A few Jim recognised from pictures he had seen or from the fish counter at his local supermarket. That was one place he liked to stand and stare at the many different colours and shapes of the unusual-sounding fish. Nearest to him was a blue barrel that had about a dozen black lobsters in it. They were all crawling round trying to be the one that ended up on top and to Jim's surprise they all had a rubber band wrapped around each big claw.

'Why have they got rubber bands on their claws?' Jim asked Gemma.

'That's so that they don't pinch the fishermen or fight each other. I'm sure they aren't worth as much if they've got legs or claws missing,' replied Gemma.

'Oh,' the young boy was not at all sure that he had been given the correct reason but he looked at Gemma, and was suddenly pleased that they were getting on with each other. She always seemed to have the answer to his questions. All the fishermen were very friendly and each found time to have a quick word with their young visitors. Gemma had evidently been before, by the way the men knew her.

Uncle Tom disappeared into the wheelhouse with Frank for a few minutes, and Jim could see through the glass that quite a heated discussion was taking place. Frank was doing a lot of pointing at Uncle Tom and then at a point away from the boat, across the harbour somewhere. Uncle Tom took off his hat and rubbed his face with his big hand. Jim didn't know his uncle very well, but he could tell that something was wrong.

Upon his return to Gemma and Jim, Uncle Tom gave no hint of the problems he was facing. 'Now, young scallywag,' he said cheerfully, 'Frank says if you fancy a trip out with him and his boys one day you would be more than welcome.'

'No thanks,' said Jim. 'I don't think I could.'

'You told me you would be sick tied up to the side Shrimp, but you've stood here happily for half an hour with no problems.'

Jim's eyes opened wide and he found he couldn't say much because his great uncle was quite right. He hadn't thought twice about stepping on board the Cornish Pride when asked. 'I don't think I'd like to take a trip out, Uncle Tom. Thanks anyway, Frank.'

Frank joined the group at the back of the boat. He still had on his shiny yellow trousers that were like a sleeveless boiler-suit which protected any clothes he wore underneath. Jim thought how he must smell of fish all the time.

They eventually said their goodbyes, and Frank sent Uncle Tom away with a large crab, wrapped in newspaper under one arm. The return journey to Jamaica Bay was a repeat of the first one with angry motorists coming and going. Once back at the house all three ate a plateful of sandwiches, which Maureen had made for them, washed down with a glass of cold lemonade. Uncle Tom retreated to his large chair on the veranda with his clay pipe, and it wasn't long before he was snoozing quietly like a sleeping bear.

'What do you fancy doing, Jim?' asked Gemma.

'I don't really know. There seems to be so much to do, it is difficult to decide what to do first.'

Again he was surprised how friendly she had become. It was good to have someone his own age to mess about with.

'Pinky!' Jim shouted. 'I'd forgotten all about him. Let's go and see him.' Both children jumped down from the table, sending a plate crashing off the table to shatter into pieces on the floor.

'Sorry, Maureen,' said Jim.

'Don't worry,' she replied in a soft voice, 'It was an accident. Go on and have some fun.'

Jim and Gemma made their way down to the cellar, where Jim bent down and picked up Pinky's box. He pushed the straw around with his fingers, the movements getting faster and faster as he realised Pinky was not in the box.

'Oh no,' said Jim with a deep sigh. He held up the shoebox with one finger poking out of a small hole that had appeared in one corner. Pinky had escaped.

'Quick, close the shutters, Jim,' shouted Gemma.

A couple of minutes later with the dull glow from the electric light throwing eerie shadows across the cellar, Gemma and Jim stepped lightly around the floor as if they were walking on eggs and doing their best not to break them. They stood and looked at each other for some time not knowing what to do.

'We'll have to go on hands and knees if we are going to look properly,' Gemma said.

'Yes, I think you're right,' agreed Jim.

Just then he spotted a brush made up of old twigs and small branches bound together onto a larger piece of wood.

'You gradually sweep the floor as I feel for Pinky with my hands,' suggested Jim.

'Okay,' said Gemma. 'Be very careful though Jim. I'll bet poor Pinky is frightened to death.'

And so they started. Jim gently moved the straw and debris with his hands until he had cleared quite a large area, and then he moved on, leaving Gemma to sweep the coal dust and dirt into a small heap. It was quite obvious that nobody had cleaned the floor for many years. As time went by, hope began to desert them. They worked their way right across the floor under the wooden stairs, and under a chute that led from the floor to a small flap next to the main cellar door. They had cleared about half of the floor when Gemma gave a yelp making Jim jump out of his skin, if that was possible.

'There he is Jim, near your left hand!' she screeched.

Jim looked down but could not see anything.

'Move forward,' instructed Gemma, 'He went towards the wall. Quickly.'

Jim moved his hands to and fro, shuffling forwards as he went. He felt sharp pieces dig into his knees but carried on regardless of his discomfort, and then suddenly what used to be a white mouse scuttled across the floor between his hands. As quick as a flash he brought his hands together round his new pet, trapping him once again.

He pulled his hands to his chest and gave Gemma a huge smile. She handed Jim an old wooden box she had found on the bench. He placed Pinky inside, and with an enormous deep breath, sat back on his legs and laughed. He looked at Gemma and when she looked at him she laughed too. They laughed and laughed until tears rolled down their faces leaving small white rivers on their blackened faces. In all the excitement neither of them had noticed they were getting very dirty making them resemble experienced coal miners. He may have suddenly changed from white to black, but at least Pinky was safe.

'We might as well continue to clear up here, Gemma. Uncle Tom would probably be quite pleased if he found it "ship-shape".'

Gemma laughed because Jim had done a very good impression of his uncle as he'd said "ship-shape". Just then Jim's expression changed.

'What's the matter?' asked Gemma.

'That's funny,' said Jim. 'I just felt a really strong draught on my face.'

'What's funny about that?' asked Gemma.

Jim looked up at her and said in a very serious voice, 'The draught came from the floor.'

Gemma knelt down beside him as Jim felt over the floor where he sat.

'There. There it is again,' he said. He held his hand a couple of inches above the floor. 'It seems to be coming through the floor in a line,' said Jim. 'Get the brush, Gemma.'

The young girl brushed the floor where Jim indicated clearing away the thick layer of mess. Both children exchanged glances quickly as they saw what they had uncovered. They were staring at a narrow gap that had appeared in the floor; it was edged with a thin piece of wood and halfway down its three-foot length was a large hook, which was set on a hinge amongst the cobbles. More sweeping revealed further gaps in the floor, and it was then that Jim and Gemma realised what they had found.

'It's a trap door,' said Jim, '— probably a secret trap door.' 'Where do you think it leads, Jim?'

'Perhaps it leads to the other side of the house,' he suggested lamely.

'Let's look,' said Gemma.

'Do you think we ought to? We should tell Uncle Tom; we don't want to get into trouble.'

'Oh Jim, it won't do any harm to have a quick look will it?'

'No, I suppose not,' replied Jim.

Using a small piece of metal lying nearby, Jim forced the hook into an upright position, and then using all his strength he began to lift. At first nothing happened, but seeing Jim struggling, Gemma added her weight to the task, and slowly the large trap door lifted up allowing a strong breeze to blow into their faces. Each going to one side, they continued to lift the door until it rested against the wall, banging against the long chain that hung from the ring. Gemma grabbed the piece of chain and attached it to the hook on the lifted panel, preventing the door from falling. Jim and Gemma stood at the side of the gaping hole breathing heavily.

'Can you smell that?' asked Gemma.

'Yes,' said Jim. 'The sea.'

Chapter 6

They stood together staring into the menacingly black hole for several minutes, both wondering what their discovery could mean, where it might lead, and what was awaiting them at the other end.

'Gemma.' Her mum called from the kitchen. 'Gemma, we've got to go now.'

'Quick,' said Gemma. 'Let's put it back and cover it up. We shouldn't tell anyone yet until we know where it goes to.' Jim agreed.

Together they struggled to replace the hatch door and hastily spread the thick cover of dirt and straw over the floor once again. Happy with the result, and with the wooden box safely in Jim's arms, both children emerged from the cellar to find Gemma's mum in the kitchen doorway.

'Oh my goodness,' said Maureen. 'What on earth have you two been up to, to get into that state? Honestly, Gemma! I'll bet that dust will stain.'

'Sorry, Mum,' she said forlornly.

'It's my fault, Maureen,' said Jim apologetically. 'Pinky ate his way out of the shoe box we'd left him in and, well you know how messy it is down there — but we did find him.'

Uncle Tom came out of the back door and started that loud laughter again. 'Well stripe me pink!' he said. 'I didn't realise we'd got visitors with us today.' His infectious laughter soon got to the other three and before long they were all helpless, holding their sides as they laughed.

'Come on, young lady,' Maureen said eventually. 'Let's get you home for a good bath. See you tomorrow, Tom. Bye, Jim.'

'Goodbye,' Jim replied. 'Oh Gemma, if you bring a torch tomorrow we'll try that little experiment with Pinky.'

'What experiment with Pinky?' replied Gemma, with a puzzled look on her face. 'Oh yes, Jim. Sorry, I'm so tired I'd forgotten about Pinky.' It sounded a lame sort of reply but a knowing look told Jim she was sure they'd got away with it. 'See you tomorrow.'

Jim took most of his clothes off, leaving them in a pile in the kitchen and walked up to the bathroom. There he had a luxuriant long shower, allowing the hot water to pour over his body making him feel relaxed and happy. He stared out of the small window that allowed the last of the day's warm glow to penetrate the steamy atmosphere. If he stood on tiptoe he could just see Uncle Tom's old garage, which stood next to the small worn path at the side of the house. It was surrounded by old trees, which swayed gently in the light breeze.

Jim had finished his shower and was towelling himself off, thinking how fresh he felt, when he heard raised voices from outside. Standing perfectly still, Jim did his best to hear what was being said. One of the voices was definitely Uncle Tom's, but the other voice was that of a much younger man. Both men were obviously upset about something, but their voices were not clear.

Jim held on to the window frame with a towel around him, straining to see what was going on. The garage doors were open, and Uncle Tom stood at the entrance with his back to the house. The younger man was in his thirties with dark hair and a very dark complexion. He was wearing a dark brown suit with a tie, and looked as if he wasn't very comfortable wearing either. It occurred to Jim that perhaps he was trying to impress his uncle. As the large stranger turned slightly, Jim was suddenly troubled at the sight of a large hammer in his right hand.

The man began pointing a finger at Uncle Tom, who in reply lifted his big fist towards the intruder. With a swift action the man ducked to his left, and with two quick movements smashed both headlights of the old Land Rover with the hammer. A great bellow came from Uncle Tom as if he wanted to awaken some ancient spirit to help him. He lunged at the man, who moved to one side, leaving the old sailor sprawling over the vehicle bonnet. As he turned round, the man in the brown suit flicked his right arm, catching Uncle Tom across the face, throwing him to the floor in a cloud of dust. Jim clearly heard the next piece of conversation.

'The next time we come, old man, it will mean big trouble. We won't mess about with you again. You've got one day, got it?'

With that, the man ran to the front of the house, and seconds later a loud powerful engine roared off leaving billowing clouds of dirt floating in the air and around where Uncle Tom still lay on the floor.

Jim threw open the bathroom door, and ran down the stairs calling as he went. 'Uncle Tom, Uncle Tom.'

As Jim reached the garage, his uncle was a pathetic sight, clawing at the garage door for a handhold to hoist himself up. He suddenly looked very, very old.

'Are you hurt? I heard what he said, Uncle Tom. He's coming back. What are you going to do? Call the police?'

'Now now, Shrimp. Don't take on so, young Jim. I'm fine. I'm fine.' Uncle Tom wiped his bloody mouth and gave his nephew a smile.

'You ought not to take any notice of a person like that Jim. They're all wind and no trousers. You mark my words; we won't see him again.'

'But what did he want?' asked Jim.

'I don't know, my lad. I think he rather fancies living here himself. But that's tough, don't you think? He should try using an estate agent.'

Uncle Tom was now on his feet dusting himself and his straw hat off. He tried to give one of his funny chuckles, but Jim could see that the smile didn't reach the old man's eyes. No, this was not something that they could just dismiss.

Very slowly, the two of them made their way back inside the house. Jim put the kettle on and silently he and his uncle sat in the kitchen, contemplating what had just happened. It seemed very strange, but Uncle Tom did not seem willing to discuss the situation. He just answered any questions Jim put to him with 'Now don't you worry, my boy' or 'Everything's fine, Jim. He won't come back.'

When Jim finally went up to the attic, he shut the window near his hammock tight as if the events of the evening had caused a sudden change in the weather. He remembered his other friend who had earlier started what might become a very exciting adventure. Pinky still looked like a black mouse as he sat in his wooden box. Very gently Jim brushed the little fellow with a piece of string that hung down from its place against the wall. Eventually Jim held a grey mouse who was eager to get back into his new home. Putting him back on the floor the boy eased himself into his hammock and thought about what was to be done the next day. It didn't worry him that he hadn't had any tea, there was too much to think about.

The following morning greeted Jim with bright sunshine. He gingerly extricated himself from his string bag and hurriedly got dressed. When he got downstairs he found Maureen preparing breakfast in the kitchen. Uncle Tom and Gemma were not about.

'Morning, Jim. Did you sleep well?' asked Maureen.

'Hello, Maureen,' Jim replied. 'Not too bad thanks.' He stopped for a second or two, and then with a worried expression on his face he said, 'Did Uncle Tom tell you what happened last night?'

Maureen stopped what she was doing, and listened with grave concern to what Jim had to say. It didn't take too long to explain the previous evening's happenings, and afterwards Maureen put her hands on Jim's shoulders and said, 'I don't know what's going on but I will have to speak to your uncle about it. Try not to think about it too much. I'm sure he knows what he is doing.' She gave Jim one of her "everything will be all right" smiles, but once again it did not hide her thoughts.

During breakfast Gemma came in with some more eggs which she had collected from the coop in the yard. Jim didn't mind that she was doing it; he didn't like the thought of being pecked by a jealous hen when taking one of her eggs.

'Hi Gemma, did you remember your torch?'

'Yes I did,' she said with a gleam in her eye.

'What are you doing today then, you two?' asked Maureen.

'Well, we thought we'd do an experiment with Pinky to see if having pink eyes is different from normal,' replied

Gemma, hoping her mum wouldn't ask any more questions.

'Oh all right. Well, don't you be cruel, will you?' said her mother.

'I promise. We won't hurt Pinky,' chipped in Jim. He had already found a great big torch in the attic. His uncle had obviously left it for him in case he needed to get out of bed in the middle of the night.

As soon as breakfast was finished Jim went to the attic and came back with the wooden box and a big piece of cardboard.

'Where is Uncle Tom?' he asked Maureen.

'I don't know, dear,' she replied. 'I wouldn't worry — he often goes out early. The Land Rover is not here; he must be running some errands. You two try not to get very dirty today. Gemma's clothes are still in soak from yesterday.'

Both children rushed out of the back door, closing it behind them to make sure that Maureen couldn't hear them.

'What's the cardboard for?' asked Gemma.

Jim had threaded a piece of string between two holes at its top to form a loop, and when he turned it over it read: "DO NOT DISTURB. DARKNESS ESSENSHAL."

'I thought we could hang this on the door to make sure we're alone,' said Jim.

'You could have spelled "essential" right,' Gemma replied.

'That doesn't matter,' said Jim. 'Let's get going.'

Once secure in the cellar, Jim put Pinky's box on the work bench. Being very careful not to get dirty, between them they lifted up the trap door, leaving some piles of dirt to re-cover it when they had finished. They shone their torches down the hole, and each gave a small shriek as the beams disappeared down some very rough looking stone steps. They were well used; each of them sloping from both sides to the middle as if hundreds of people had used them in the past. Judging by the covering of cobwebs, no human had passed this way for years. Both children shivered as a feeling of great excitement coursed through their veins.

'Are you ready?' said Gemma.

'I think so,' replied Jim.

'Shouldn't we take anything with us? You know, just in case,' asked Gemma.

Jim put his torch down and emptied his pockets into both hands. 'Let's see,' he said. 'I've got some string, a whistle, a safety pin, a pencil and some paper, a long piece of blue towelling and a small bar of chocolate my mum gave me.'

Gemma was impressed with her new friend but didn't say anything. With all Jim's bits and pieces safely installed in his pockets they decided it was time to go.

Inspecting the entrance more closely, the children found a drop of about three feet to the first step. Jim cleared away all the cobwebs with a twig from the cellar floor and decided to take it with them.

He dropped down first, and shone his torch down the narrow passageway. He could see the steps disappear very gently to the right after about fifteen metres.

'It looks pretty dry,' he informed Gemma. 'I think we will be okay.'

'Shouldn't we just tell Mum what we're going to do?' suggested Gemma.

'Do you think your mum would let us go down here by ourselves? I don't think she would. We are only going to have a quick look. I'll bet we'll be gone for a matter of minutes — come on.'

Without further protest, Gemma dropped down onto the first step and cautiously followed Jim into the tunnel. Being small helped, for the tunnel at its beginning was only just big enough for the children to walk along, bent over double. The tunnel itself was very clean with the sides almost smooth. After only a minute of moving slowly along the cold stone tube, both children stopped and listened, there was a distant rumble that came and went in short bursts.

'What's that noise?' Gemma asked.

'I'm not sure,' replied Jim. 'But that smell is still very strong, it may well be the sea we can hear.'

'I'm scared,' whispered Gemma.

'So am I, but if we think about it there's no real need to be worried is there? It's fairly obvious that nobody has been down here for years so we won't bump into anyone will we?'

'No, I suppose not.' Gemma was still concerned but they both began moving again. Very gradually the slope of the tunnel levelled out and the steps disappeared altogether. The ceiling got lower as well, until Jim and Gemma were sitting backwards pushing themselves along with their hands and feet. The sound they had heard earlier was becoming a booming echo as they got closer. There was no doubt now that it was the sea they could hear.

It was becoming more and more difficult to shine their torches in front of them as they scurried forwards.

'Stop,' said Jim. He was feeling with his left hand along the side wall of the tunnel.

'What's the matter Jim?' asked Gemma.

'There's another tunnel here,' Jim exclaimed.

'Where?' asked Gemma. She leant forward and shone her torch towards where Jim was investigating. Sure enough, another, bigger, tunnel branched off to the left. Its sides were a lot rougher as if they had been man-made, whereas the tunnel the children were in was obviously made by natural means. Only three or four feet into this second tunnel, there was a blockage that covered the hole in its entirety. This too was definitely man-made and was created from what looked like the top of a very big barrel, wedged into place. Jim pushed against it, but it was as solid as the rock in which it was wedged.

'Never mind that, Jim, I think we are getting quite close to the end of this tunnel. Turn off your torch for a minute,' said Gemma.

Jim did as he was asked. For a while the children couldn't see anything in the pitch blackness, but as their eyes became accustomed to the dark a very faint glow showed itself in front of them.

'There,' said Gemma. 'I told you. Let's get going.'

On the two went, forgetting any fears they may have had as the thought of what lay ahead took over. Within a couple of minutes the passageway began to get significantly larger, allowing Jim and Gemma to stand up. The light got stronger and stronger, and the noise of the booming surf got louder and louder, until suddenly without any warning the tunnel opened up into a cave.

The two small children stopped and stared about them in awe. They had emerged onto a type of stone platform which was completely flat and about two and a half metres wide at one end, tapering to nothing as it disappeared into the cave wall. Alongside the platform was a bright greeny blue pool of seawater which had free passage into the cavern by the massive opening which arched a metre high above the tossing water. There were jagged rocks all around the cave floor, particularly at its entrance, leaving enough room only for a small rowing boat to get through.

Jim could see bright sunshine through the opening, which filtered through the water, lighting up the cave. The open sea could not be seen because of a wall of rock which covered the cave's entrance.

'Wow,' said Gemma. 'What have we found?'

'I don't know,' Jim replied, 'but something tells me we are going to have to find out. I wonder if you can see this from the open water.'

'It's doubtful,' whispered Gemma. 'It doesn't look as if it has been used for years and years. Look above you, Jim.'

Jim looked up to see a hole in the ceiling above the platform. There was bright sunshine showing inside where it twisted round to its left. There were some very sharp-looking rocks sticking out at peculiar angles from the sides.

'Do you think you could give me a leg up there?' Jim asked Gemma.

'It's only a couple of metres — we should be able to manage. Be careful though, Jim. Those rocks look very sharp.'

With a big smile Jim took out the blue towel from his pocket. 'I knew some of this stuff would be useful,' he chuckled.

Gemma cupped her hands together and put her back against the side of the cave and allowed Jim to hoist himself into the hole. It was a very comfortable fit, giving him plenty of room to move his limbs. The sharp rocks made good foot and handholds. Using the towel to protect his fingers from the hard points he quickly climbed to near the top. As he got closer the tunnel became almost vertical and each handhold began to hurt. Finally he threw the towel over the edge onto some razor-sharp rocks, and using all his strength he pulled himself up and up, until the top of his head was bathed in sunshine. Suddenly his fingers lost their grip, and he slipped from his perch just managing to throw his legs out, saving himself on another angular rock.

'Are you all right?' called Gemma.

'Yes, I think so,' replied Jim, apparently no worse for the slip. Unfortunately he had to descend without the help of his towel as it had snagged on the rocks as he slipped, leaving it flapping at the hole's entrance. He eventually found himself dangling from the other end of the tunnel much to Gemma's relief.

'Well done, Jim,' she cried slapping him joyfully on the back. 'What could you see? Tell me.'

'I didn't see much at all. I should say there was nothing to see. The hole comes out on the cliff face, quite high above the sea. There's nothing there at all.'

'There's something I spotted while you were gone,' said Gemma. 'There are some big metal rings for mooring boats. Look — one just here, and one on the opposite side of the cave.'

Jim got onto his knees and craned his neck over the platform. There, firmly planted into the rock, was a rusty metal ring about the size of a dinner plate. Its twin was almost exactly opposite, five metres away, just above the water line. Jim looked at the water and thought it was probably only a few feet deep.

He remembered the twig he had picked up from his uncle's cellar. Rolling his shirtsleeve up, he lay on the platform and plunged the twig into the cold clear water. He waved it around and then pulled it out again.

'Well,' he said looking at his wet arm with its extension. 'It's deeper than that,' although he didn't really know what difference the depth of water should make 'We ought to be getting back.'

'Isn't it exciting?' Gemma's eyes shone in the weird light.

'Look!' cried Jim. 'The tide is still coming in. There's hardly any gap between the sea and the mouth of the cave.' Sure enough the tide was coming in, but a look round the cave revealed a dark line which indicated the high water level just underneath the platform's edge.

'If you wanted to come ashore from a boat or bring things from a boat without people seeing you, wouldn't this be perfect?'

'Yes,' agreed Gemma. 'I wonder who else knows about it though, Jim. Come on — let's go.'

Picking up their torches both children entered the tunnel and slid and scrambled up to where the steps began again. Within a few minutes Jim had reached the cellar of his great uncle's house and, closely followed by Gemma, they climbed out of the tunnel. Once again being careful not to get even dirtier they replaced the trap door and covered up their exciting secret.

'How do you fancy going fishing tomorrow?' enquired Jim.

'Fishing? Huh. It's not exactly my idea of fun,' Gemma replied.

'No, I mean proper fishing, with Frank. He must bring the Cornish Pride this way up the coast!'

'Great idea, Jim.' Once again her eyes shone in the dim glow from the electric light.

When was the last time this cave had been used? More importantly who had used it and why? Where was this adventure going to lead them?

Chapter 7

Uncle Tom didn't mention to Jim where he had been that day, but when he heard his nephew's request to go fishing on the Cornish Pride with Frank, he raised his bushy eyebrows and a smile spread across his tanned features.

'Well, you young scallywag. You've changed your tune suddenly. What's brought this on then, eh?'

'I don't know,' Jim said, 'I talked to Gemma and we sort of thought it might be fun.'

If his great uncle was watching Jim's eyes closely, he may well have guessed something was afoot, but without further questioning, Uncle Tom made all the arrangements for the following day.

That night Jim had great difficulty sleeping. He was wrestling with this strange idea he'd developed that the nasty visitor of the previous evening may have something to do with the secret tunnel. But why?

The next day dawned very much like the previous two days with blazing sunshine, and that carefree holiday atmosphere around Jamaica Bay. Jim and Gemma ate a hearty breakfast on the instructions of Uncle Tom, and once finished they climbed into the Land Rover. Jim noticed the headlights were restored to working order and the noise of the engine wasn't so bad, with hardly any smoke coming from the exhaust.

The old man looked at Jim and winked. 'She's running better now I've had her looked at, don't you reckon, Shrimp?' The boy agreed it would be much less embarrassing.

'Hey, you two, jump in the back. I'm coming with you,' Maureen called. So Jim and Gemma climbed into the open back and hung on for dear life as the old machine rattled and bumped out onto the track.

The journey to the dock was completely uneventful; no clouds of blue smoke, no honking vehicles and no angry drivers. Uncle Tom still smiled to himself and he still tapped his hand on the steering wheel as if he was enjoying a jolly tune from his radio.

When they arrived at the water's edge, the Cornish Pride was waiting with a smiling crew ready to help their visitors on board. The children turned around and waved at the old man in the straw hat and the kind-looking woman who stood next to him as the small fishing boat pushed its nose into the narrow channel and headed out to sea.

'See you around three o'clock if the tide's right!' shouted Frank. Uncle Tom lifted up both thumbs in recognition of his message, as the boat disappeared around the harbour wall.

Jim watched the ship's master, Frank Penhaligon, as he eased his pride and joy around the moored boats and navigation buoys. Thick black smoke belched from the boat's exhaust and the engine picked up its rhythm as the first heavy roller lifted it easily and then dropped it gently like a giant handling a delicate child's toy. Although Frank continually sucked on an old battered pipe clenched between his teeth, he rarely put his lighter to it. His thick brown hair moved in the sea air as he stood casually against the cabin's door. He had a very red complexion, as if he were continually embarrassed, and long thick sideburns that grew lower than his ears. He had striking eyes that shone like two pieces of wet coal and gave life to his face. His water-and-fish-proof overtrousers covered his thick seagoing jumper and checked shirt.

'You'll have to do exactly as I tell you, young 'uns,' he called over. 'Things can get quite tricky if the weather changes quickly or the nets snag, so make sure you listen carefully, right?'

Both children nodded vigorously as Nobby the youngest of the crew shouted, 'Don't worry, skip — we can always use 'em as bait if they cause us any problems.'

This made them all laugh. Nobby was obviously Frank's son as he looked like a twin of him except for his weathered face. His clothes were very similar as well. Tony, a man in his thirties, was busy making good some holes in a lobster pot. He too was biting on a pipe, and Jim thought that if he tightened his jaw any more the

71

pipe would snap. He didn't say much, and always seemed miles away with his thoughts.

The other member of the crew was Bob Smith, still quite a young man who obviously loved life as a fisherman. He was only too willing to show Jim and Gemma a piece of equipment or how a particular operation was carried out.

Jim was quite surprised at how well he felt. He was so busy looking at things that he didn't feel in the least bit ill. Gemma seemed to be the same. They left Pentilrock far behind and continued steaming out to sea.

Bob told the children exactly what they would be doing, how they had more than fifty sites to visit. At each site they had to check the lobster pot that was attached to a marker buoy that floated on the sea's surface. The boat usually travelled a total of twenty miles each day in the quest for delicious lobsters that would go as far afield as London to be sold.

After a pleasant cruise, Frank brought the boat to a stop next to a bright orange ball that floated effortlessly over each wave. Nobby and Bob caught the ball with a boat hook, and together they pulled up the rope, coiling the slimy length in big hoops as they went, to avoid getting it twisted and in knots. After a minute or so a big black basket appeared, cascading water over the deck. At first Jim thought their effort was in vain, but then he noticed something moving in the bottom of the basket, as Nobby plunged his hand into a small hole on the top.

He pulled out a very large crab that waved its big pincer arms about menacingly. Bob got a large piece of fish from a bucket and put it on a small pin inside the basket, which was once again thrown over board where it was closely followed by the snaking rope. The orange ball flipped up and over the side and then remained stationary, anchored by the heavy lobster pot.

The boat moved a couple of hundred metres to the next buoy, and the crab was put in a large tray nailed to the boat's bottom, with its claws wrapped up with rubber bands. It was all tremendously exciting for the children and they were even allowed to help pull in the odd basket or throw one back over the side.

'Why do the stupid things climb in, and why don't they climb out again?' asked Gemma.

Tony was still repairing lobster pots on the deck and he said, 'You see this rubber sleeve which surrounds the entrance hole?' He pointed to a tube which was the only way in or out of the trap. 'The lobster, or whatever smells the fish we put in the baskets, eventually works out that it can only get to its free meal through the tube. Getting in is no problem for a crab or a lobster but because the tube is smooth and sits above the floor of the cage, the poor little crustaceans can't grab hold of anything to pull themselves out so they have to wait around until we come along and get them out.'

This was the most Tony had said, and he seemed pleased to have imparted the information to two such willing pupils. The day continued in much the same vein, with Jim and Gemma helping out wherever possible. Frank still controlled the boat from the little wheel house and Jim thought it was about time to go and have a quiet word with him while Gemma was busy helping Tony.

'Did you hear about the trouble we had at Jamaica Bay the other night, Frank?' asked Jim casually.

'I sure did. It must have scared you a bit, Jim,' replied Frank.

'It did a bit, but I couldn't do much to help. I was having a shower,' said Jim.

'Now you listen here. I know the type of person who called on your Uncle Tom the other night, and you are to promise me that if anything like that happens again you will keep out of the way. They'd not think twice about hurting you or anyone else. I only wish there was a way I could help, but your uncle's place is so far away,' pondered Frank.

'There's always his ship's whistle or foghorn or whatever it is. Surely that's loud enough for anyone to hear,' suggested Jim.

'I don't know,' replied Frank. 'You could always try it if you are desperate. There is the phone of course, but the lines are down quite a lot round here for various reasons. Whatever you do though, Jim, remember what I've said.'

Silence fell over the wheel house, when Jim noticed some charts spread over a board at Frank's side. He peered at them curiously.

'Uncle Tom's got some maps like this. Whereabouts is Jamaica Bay, then, Frank?'

Frank put a light pencil mark on a cliff and indicated it to Jim.

'I'll bet there are quite a few caves round here in the cliffs, aren't there, Frank?' asked Jim.

'Yes, there certainly are, Jim. They've been used for all sorts of things over the years. Most of them have either been destroyed or sealed up now. They've proved to be more trouble than they are worth,' said Frank.

'Do we have to go near Jamaica Bay?' asked Jim.

'Well, not normally, young Jim. Why?' replied Frank.

The boy looked sheepishly at the skipper and said, 'Oh I just wondered what it looked like from the sea, that's all.'

'Well, as it's your first trip out with me I'll make an exception and go back closer in than we normally would. In fact we'll be about there in thirty minutes or so.'
Frank's face broke into a smile as Jim rushed from the small cabin to speak to his young friend,

Jim told Gemma that Frank was going to sail near to Jamaica Bay, and it would be a good chance to see if their newly discovered secret was visible from the open water. The boat steamed nearer to the cliffs, and suddenly Gemma tugged at Jim's arm.

'Look, there's your uncle's house, Jim. See the trees?'

The boy scanned the cliffs until his eyes settled on the old wooden house that seemed to be perched on the very edge of the cliff, liable to fall off at any minute.

'Can you see it?' called Frank. 'Or do you want to borrow my bins?'

'Bins?' asked Jim.

'Binoculars,' laughed Frank.

'Oh yes, great. Thanks,' replied Jim. He had great difficulty at first keeping the lenses steady with the swaying motion of the sea, but the cliff instantly jumped into focus revealing the many colours of the ancient rocks. He managed to focus on the old house and then steadily followed the cliff down, immediately below the house.

He drew in a sharp breath as there on the rocks, apparently abandoned, was his blue towel. He carried on down the cliff but the picture he saw gave him no indication there was a cave or even a small inlet thereabouts. Jim called to Gemma and let her scan the cliffs just as he had. From her reaction Jim knew that she too had seen his blue towel. She moved the binoculars about and then, satisfied, gave them back to Frank.

'Happy then?' he asked.

'Very, thanks,' replied Jim. 'Thanks very much for letting us come out with you. It has been great.'

'No problem,' said the fisherman. The other three crew members were busy tidying up the mess caused by their constant work. By the time they reached the quayside, the barrels were full and the fishermen seemed happy with their work. Uncle Tom was waiting for Jim and Gemma, and they all said their good-byes.

'Don't forget what I said, Jim,' called Frank.

'I won't. Thanks.'

They hurriedly told Uncle Tom what they had spent their day doing, while the old man listened in silence. The journey seemed much shorter to Jim, and once back at the house their dinner was ready: casseroled lamb with spicy dumplings.

'Another piece of real home cooking,' Jim was informed by his old uncle. He forgot to mention the fact that Maureen was still in attendance and had probably dealt with dinner unaided by Uncle Tom.

'Oh by the way, Shrimp, a letter came for you today. I'd forgotten all about it.' He handed Jim the letter, and watched as the boy tore it open and did his best to read it.

'It's from Mum and Dad,' he announced. 'Mum has had her operation, and everything seems to be okay. She's to stay in hospital for another two weeks before she goes home.'

'Well that is good news, Shrimp. Didn't we tell you not to worry? You see, she'll be back to her old self when you go home,' cried Uncle Tom.

'Yes, I hope so,' said Jim softly. 'Would you mind if I went to your study and wrote to Dad, just to let him know I'm okay?'

'Course you can. You don't have to ask. Paper, pens and envelopes are all there,' replied the old man.

'We'll say goodnight,' called Maureen. 'See you first thing in the morning. I'm glad about your mum.'

Jim slipped behind the desk and wrote a short note explaining all he'd done — well, almost all he'd done — and the fact that he was having a really great time, — oh, and about Pinky. By the time he had completed it he found Uncle Tom sitting on the veranda smoking his long clay pipe. They sat for a few moments together in silence.

'It's about time you went off to sling your hook, young Shrimp,' joked the genial giant.

Jim didn't object as he had begun to feel completely worn out when he'd sat next to his uncle.

'Goodnight Uncle Tom,' he said. 'And thanks for being here when I need you.' He suddenly flung his arms around the massive shoulders and gave as big a squeeze as he could.

'That's all right, Jim. It's nice to have you around. You brighten the place up you know,' replied the old man.

Jim went to bed too tired to think, and fell into a deep and dreamless sleep. He awoke with a start to the noise of banging and shouting and the great shaggy beard of his uncle looming close to his face.

'Quick, Jim. Get up, get up, boy! There's a fire! Grab a top and shoes. Jump about, lad!' Uncle Tom was in a state.

'Where is the fire, uncle?' asked Jim quickly.

'The garage, boy. We need help. The blasted phone is out again.'

'Ring your siren, Uncle, that loud whistle,' suggested Jim.

'Good idea lad.' With that, both of them ran downstairs to the old man's land-bound bridge, and Uncle Tom slapped a button attached to the wall. The loud screeching noise that pierced the night air like a scream seemed unbearable to Jim, even with his ears covered.

'Downstairs, lad. Quick.'

Outside, the air was alive with sparks and crackles as the wooden garage burned ferociously. With a loud bang the back of the old Land Rover reared up as its petrol tank exploded, causing a huge piece of the metal to fly through the air, landing in front of the house with a slap and a hiss. The boy and his uncle could only stand and watch, hoping that the fire wouldn't spread to the house. Very soon sirens could be heard as Pentilrock fire engine sped into the clearing, followed shortly by a small police car. The ship's whistle had turned itself off after two minutes, but it certainly seemed to have done its job.

'Tom?' came a voice from the conservatory area. 'Are you okay?'

It was Maureen and Gemma. They had heard the whistle and seen the flames, but had had to cut round the back of the house because the path ran next to the garage.

'How did it happen?' asked Maureen.

'I don't know, girl,' said Uncle Tom, 'I heard a bang and came out. Must have been faulty wiring on them new lights.'

They stood in silence as another car came into the light of the fire. It was Frank. As he got out of the vehicle he looked questioningly at Tom.

'Don't you start,' Tom said.

'I heard the whistle, Jim,' said Frank with a wink and a thumbs up. Jim nodded, too bewildered to take in what was happening. The firemen had the fire out in no time at all, but continued to "damp down", as the chief fire officer had said, "just in case". The relief was that there was no damage to the house. Maureen made huge pots of coffee for everyone while Tom stood talking to the police and fire officers with Frank. When all the coffee had been consumed, the firemen disappeared, and the local police sergeant, Colin Mineards, told Uncle Tom he would be back first thing next day. Only then did Jim realise it was two o'clock in the morning. Had the fire been caused by the new lights on the Land Rover or was there a more sinister explanation?

There was certainly a lot to find out.

Chapter 8

Jim couldn't sleep much that night. He lay in his hammock thinking about all the things that had happened since he arrived in Cornwall. It seemed like weeks, although it was still only a few days. He decided that he should press his Uncle Tom to discover as much as possible about the unwanted visitors and also some sort of history about Jamaica Bay. Perhaps the answers he was looking for lay there.

As soon as Jim heard noises from downstairs he got up, even though it was still very early. He found his uncle in his room with the door open.

'Morning, lad. Couldn't sleep either, eh? I'm just going to take the morning bearings — care to join me on the bridge?' The boy gave a big smile and followed his uncle into his special room above the conservatory. On one of the benches was a large book in which Jim's uncle made various notes: temperature, barometer reading, the wind's direction, and the wind speed reading from a funny windmill-type thing that looked like four egg cups attached to a rod outside the window. Jim also looked with great interest at a list on the wall of local high tide times. For that week high tide was about midday, receding by about half an hour or so daily. That made low tide about 6.00 p.m. He had already decided that a thorough investigation of the cave had to be made, and low tide was the best time to do it.

Uncle Tom, with a pair of binoculars to his eyes, was surveying the coastline as a king might look over his kingdom.

'How do you think the garage caught fire last night, Uncle Tom? I mean these things don't just happen do they?' The boy waited for his uncle to reply.

'Well now, lad, I don't want you bothering yourself over a silly thing like that. I should imagine that fool of a mechanic wired up the lights wrong, causing a short-out. I shall go and see him today and bend his ear for him,' replied the old man.

'You don't think it had anything to do with the man that came the other night, do you?' asked Jim quickly, hardly daring to expect the old man to remain calm.

'Now don't you dare mention that again, Jim.' He had swung around and thrust his face towards the boy, appearing threatening for the first time. Just as quickly as he'd turned angry he seemed to shrink away and appear hurt.

'I'm sorry, Jim. It's wrong of me to fly off the handle at you for no reason. I'm just a bit worried about things right now. I'm sure there is a reasonable explanation for all this.'

Jim went on: 'But what did that man really want, and why did he say you only had a day to decide?'

Just then there was a heavy knock from downstairs.

'I'll talk to you later, Jim. I bet that's the police.'

Uncle Tom rushed down the stairs and, as predicted, found Sergeant Mineards at the door. They went into the study. Try as he might, Jim couldn't quite hear what was being said. He went into the kitchen and put the kettle on to boil. Who had ever heard of a policeman not wanting a cup of tea? Jim sat down with a bowl of cereal and waited for his uncle to come through, which he did after a couple of minutes.

'Oh well done, Jim. I was just coming to make the tea. It would appear we are going to be a bit overrun with some of Sergeant Mineards' colleagues this morning. Perhaps it might be an idea for you to go to Gemma's while all this is going on. Would that be okay?'

As he had a mouthful of soggy wheaty flakes, Jim nodded his head. He would enjoy having a look at Gemma's house. It was only a few hundred metres away, and Jim wondered why he hadn't seen it before. Gemma and her mum arrived shortly afterwards and Maureen readily agreed to take the children back to her house.

'I think the telephone engineers are coming this morning anyway,' she said. 'I hope they can finally sort out this mess they call a telephone exchange! We seem to be without a phone more than we are with it.'

They said goodbye to the old man and went outside. The old garage was now just a pile of burnt wood and ashes, with the chassis of the Land Rover sitting sadly amongst the ruins. As they stepped between the pieces of debris, a blue car pulled up with three men inside. They were obviously policemen by the look of them, and all three began to put on white boiler suits as soon as they had got out of the vehicle, like eager decorators.

Maureen and the two children walked slowly along the hard dirt path which was bordered on both sides by bushes and tall trees. Jim imagined that during the winter months and bad weather this path would be almost impassable. There was no grass or gravel, only bare tree roots and mud, at present baked hard by the sun. The walk took only five minutes. Gemma's house was a single storey cottage with a thatched roof. The walls were a dirty white colour with dark wooden beams set above the doors and windows, and occasionally there were vertical beams for support.

The garden was a mass of colourful flowers and small bushy plants, with a stone path that led to the front door in the centre of the building. It was totally surrounded by trees at the rear, but in front of the house the land opened up to allow the front garden to establish itself. It looked a very homely, "lived-in" place in which, Jim thought, anyone could be happy. As they walked up the old path he noticed a small thatched roof to the right of the cottage.

'What's that?' he called, pointing to the strange structure.

'It's an old well,' replied Gemma. 'I don't think it's had water in for donkey's years but it's nice to look at. We'll have a closer look later if you like.'

Once inside, it was immediately noticeable that the ceilings were very low, and the doorways were much lower than in any house Jim had known before. The walls must have been three feet thick with each window being very deep set, casting weird shadows in every room. The cottage was only one room wide with each room connected to the next by a door.

'What a strange little house,' said Jim. 'I've never seen anything like it before. How old is it, Maureen?'

'Oh, at least 250 years. It's only recently had water and electricity fitted, but it suits Gemma and me, doesn't it sweetie?'

Gemma nodded with a big smile on her face. She obviously liked it.

Jim really enjoyed his time at Gemma's house. He was particularly fascinated by the well at the side of the house. Gemma shone a torch down the dark hole but it didn't penetrate the blackness. Jim dropped a small stone down and it took three seconds to hit the bottom. The brickwork at the head of the well had been rebuilt fairly recently as it looked new, not aged like the house. The other strange thing Jim noticed was that about four feet down the well there was a brick missing, as if it had fallen away because of frosty weather, but none of the others were like it. He didn't mention it though.

On the way back to Jamaica Bay he looked as if he was acting rather stupid, taking long, giant steps, stretching them as long as they'd go.

'What on earth are you doing Jim?' said Gemma. When there was no reply, she copied Jim so that the two of them looked like astronauts walking on the moon. His mind always seemed to be working overtime, and it would have taken far too much effort to tell Gemma he was measuring the distance between the two buildings. As on the previous night, Maureen decided to skirt round the back of the house because of the white-suited policemen who had gathered in a group around the ruins of the garage. Jim left Gemma and her mum going into the house and then ran back to the side of the house nearest to the impromptu police conference.

Sergeant Mineards was talking. 'Are you sure, David? There can be no doubt then?'

'No, sarge. There was definitely an accelerant used, probably petrol by the look of the stains left on the remains of a bottle we found. There can be no doubt. We checked the electrics in the car like Tom suggested, but in my opinion they are in perfect condition. The fire was started deliberately, using a bottle of petrol with a burning rag stuffed into the top of it.'

There was silence after the officer had finished while the sergeant made a few notes.

'Okay lads, I'll see you all back at the station later. I've got a few questions to ask here. He must be keeping something from us.'

Jim ran back round to the back door and went into the kitchen where his Uncle Tom, Maureen and Gemma were sitting at the kitchen table talking.

'Hi, Shrimp,' cried Jim's uncle. 'What's bugging you then? You look like you're looking for a fight.'

'Have the police spoken to you yet?' asked Jim.

'No, not yet. Why?' replied the old man.

'Listen, Uncle. You must tell them what happened the other night. I think it may be very important.'

'You worry too much boy,' replied Uncle Tom. 'I'm sure that wiring caused the fire.'

'I'm sorry to have to tell you this, but you are wrong.' Sergeant Mineards had come in through the open front door and made his way into the kitchen. 'The fire was started deliberately, probably by a "Molotov cocktail", a fire bomb. I think you and I need to have a chat, don't you? I'll wait in the study.' He turned and disappeared down the hallway.

'Well,' said Uncle Tom. 'There's a turn up! You may well be right, Jim. I'm going to have to tell him.'

For the second time in as many days, Uncle Tom looked as if his years had caught up with him. He walked slowly down the hallway to impart his information to Sergeant Mineards. Maureen prepared the evening meal and the children hung around doing nothing in particular. Uncle Tom spent two hours talking to the policeman and when he finally emerged his features looked strained and tired.

They all sat around the large table and ate their meal in silence. Nobody felt like talking. When the dishes were cleared away, Uncle Tom got his long clay pipe and sucked on it thoughtfully without putting a match to the little bowl.

'I think it's about time I filled you in on what's been happening and why I think Jamaica Bay has suddenly attracted a lot of attention,' he said.

The other three pulled their chairs closer to the table in anticipation of a long story.

'Now, some of the things I'm going to say Maureen and Gemma will know already, so if you two can bear with me, I'm sure Jim would like to know the whole story.

Jamaica Bay hasn't always been called Jamaica Bay. That's a name I invented so as to remind me of my time in the West Indies. No. Many years ago it was a well-known house. How long did it lie empty, Maureen?'

'Oh, about twenty years, I think. Certainly before we came,' she replied.

'I've only found this out since I've been here,' continued the old man, 'but this was once called "Smugglers Rest". Why, I don't know, but there we are.'

Jim and Gemma exchanged glances and a bolt of excitement suddenly landed in the children's stomachs.

Uncle Tom went on. 'It used to be owned by a man called "Slater". He lived his life as a virtual recluse with hardly any visitors. He was never seen in the village, not even in the shops. Nobody knew anything about him. It was rumoured that he did a lot of business abroad on the Continent, but nobody had any idea what sort of business he dealt in or with whom he conducted it.

'Now, I remember quite distinctly many many years ago, a daring robbery took place in Amsterdam. It made headline news all over the world. A set of diamonds worth millions and millions of pounds was stolen. It was the national treasure. The Dutch were up in arms. The police left no stone unturned but for months nothing was discovered, until one day, quite by accident, a man was arrested for a very minor offence in London. Upon searching his vehicle, police found the stolen Amsterdam diamonds concealed in the back seat. That man was Slater. The one thing that really baffled the police was the single diamond which formed the centrepiece of the whole collection. Its name was "The White Tiger", a massive stone, and it was not with the others when Slater was arrested. It was said to be worth over two million pounds even then. In court it was proved that Slater was on his way to sell the diamonds, and he was given a long prison sentence. In fact he should still be in prison now.'

'You mean he escaped?' said Gemma.

'No, girl, he died in his prison cell. He had a massive heart attack, and the secret of The White Tiger went to the grave with him — or so everyone thought.

'Now, where do I come into the picture you may ask yourself. I made quite a bit of money from being a sailor with my own boat out in the West Indies, always busy. But I wasn't getting any younger and I decided to sell my business and invest everything in London on some advice from "friends" I thought I had. Well, after a couple of years I found out that my money was disappearing. It had not been properly looked after for me and the only way to keep an eye on it was to come back to England. Being a seafaring man, I liked the idea of the Cornish coast. This place was up for rent so I took it. Old Slater being in prison hung on to it for as long as he could but he wasn't doing any deals and surprisingly enough he still had a mortgage on it. So the bank took possession of the place, but because of Slater nobody seemed to want it. That's why it was empty for so long, Maureen. It's no palace but I really like it here — if I ever get my investments back I'll buy it.

'So how does that involve you with the Slater business?' asked Maureen.

'Well, just after I got here I began to get the odd letter telling me to get out or else. Anonymous of course. The letters became more frequent and more and more threatening. Then a few days ago as you all know we had a little visit from that chap. He wants us out.'

'Who is he then, Uncle Tom?' asked Jim.

'Funnily enough,' said the old man, 'his name is "Slater" too, but he is Mr Slater Junior, who wants to take possession of Jamaica Bay, rather quickly it seems. It's obvious there's something here that he wants, but I've had the place turned upside down and I can't find anything. I even took the cellar apart but that hasn't been disturbed for years.'

Again Jim and Gemma exchanged an excited glance.

Uncle Tom went on: 'I've got to be honest with you, I've had a belly full of young Slater already and if I don't get my money back I won't be able to afford to stay here. It's not looking too good.'

'Do you think Slater knows where to look for whatever it is that's here?' asked Gemma.

'I don't think he can do,' said the old man. 'The place is deserted quite a lot of the time. He could have come in and taken it any time. Imagine, though, if I'm sat on The White Tiger and I don't even know it!'

The thought appeared to amuse him as he sat rocking silently in his chair.

'Well, all I ask,' said Maureen, 'is that you two take care. There's no telling what this man Slater might do if he doesn't get his way.'

'I don't think we need to worry now,' said Uncle Tom. 'The police have got all the details. It won't take long to run him to ground. Don't worry, girl.'

Maureen and Gemma soon left the house, and Jim said goodnight to his uncle. He now knew all there was to know except what was hidden at Jamaica Bay and where exactly it was. But as he stared out at the night sky through his open window, he had a big smile on his face as he thought to himself he had a pretty good idea where to look.

Chapter 9

Jim was very excited. He sat patiently at the breakfast table trying not to appear rude as Maureen put a plate of eggs and bacon in front of him. He wasn't really hungry, but without knowing what lay in store for him later in the day, he thought he may as well eat it thankfully.

He hadn't had a chance to speak to Gemma alone yet, but he only had to look at her to know she shared his excitement. There had to be a good chance that the secret tunnel was hiding The White Tiger, and there was also a good chance that only Gemma and Jim knew anything about it. One thing that did puzzle Jim was the existence of the blocked off tunnel — where could it run to? His thoughts were interrupted by Maureen.

'Now you two, Uncle Tom has gone to Newquay with Frank this morning, and he asked me to get you both to do something with the old garage. Frank's taken the old Land Rover away and Uncle Tom wants the whole thing tidying up. I thought if you can carry any bits there to the driveway, we'll have a good old bonfire.'

It wasn't exactly Jim's idea of a good day but he agreed to help, if only to cheer up his uncle who appeared to be feeling really fed up. What with the events of the day before, who could blame him? Maureen found the children a pair of old gardening gloves each and went with them to the ruins of the wooden garage. It reminded Jim of pictures he'd seen about World War 2; how whole buildings were reduced to ashes with only a corner of the structure remaining upright to prove a building had once stood there.

Apart from a couple of roof timbers which hadn't really burnt much, there were no large pieces to carry. A wheelbarrow was ample for any pieces left. As soon as the children had made a large pile of burnt wood, Maureen poked some old newspaper into its base and lit it. In only a couple of minutes the fire engulfed the wood, crackling and spitting like a big joint roasting in the oven.

The children continued ferrying the remains of the garage to the bonfire, and Maureen added them to the pyre. Within two hours Jim was using the yard brush to sweep up the small ashes leaving four square holes in the ground where the corner posts of the garage stood. It didn't have a concrete base like most garages.

It gave Jim a nice feeling when he looked at the clean earth, where earlier there was a mass of charred wood and ashes making quite an eyesore. Even the bonfire was dying now, showing a circle of grey powder leaving no sign of the mass of timber they had burnt.

'There now,' said Maureen. 'Your Uncle Tom will be really pleased with the morning's work, don't you think?' The three of them stood casually leaning on their brooms or shovels like resting builder's labourers.

'I'm sure he will,' agreed Jim.

Just then an engine came into earshot from the track. No, two engines. The first was a Land Rover painted in pillar box red, the second was a vehicle recovery wagon. The Land Rover swung round in an arc and then reversed towards the site of the old garage with Uncle Tom at the wheel. It parked with great care between the four holes in the ground. It wasn't difficult to imagine the garage still intact around the bright red vehicle. Frank got out of the recovery vehicle and joined the other three looking on with amusement at Uncle Tom. He too got out of the Land Rover, and when he realised everyone was watching him, he said, 'Well, we can't be without wheels now, can we? I asked Frank to get rid of the other one, and he kindly offered to take me to buy another one. I know it's not new but it'll certainly do me for a while.'

They all went inside the house and had tea and sandwiches. The morning's work must have built up a good appetite because Maureen had to make more. Just then there was a heavy knock at the door. Uncle Tom opened it and was followed back into the kitchen by Sergeant Mineards, who sat down and gratefully accepted a mug of coffee. It was some time and two sandwiches later that the policeman took up the pad he had bought with him and turned back to Uncle Tom with an official look on his face.

'As you know, Tom, this character Slater has already committed some serious crimes against you, and we have enough proof for him to be arrested and charged. He's probably looking at a lengthy prison sentence. You know what they say, like father like son. We have one major problem though. Richard Slater seems to have disappeared without trace,' Sergeant Mineards went on: 'His home address is empty, and our information tells us he has probably gone into hiding.'

'Oh dear,' said Uncle Tom. 'That makes things rather difficult. Where do we go from here, Colin?'

'Well,' said the policeman, 'I've given it a great deal of thought. It's difficult to know what to do for the best, but to my way of thinking, if we remove the object of his desire then that will stop him from trying to get hold of Jamaica Bay. After all, if there's no treasure to be had what is the point?'

'That's all very well,' argued the old sailor, 'but how are you going to do that?'

The sergeant breathed a heavy sigh and went on. 'It will take a lot of help from you, Tom, but if you agree I can get a team in and take this place apart, just to make sure it's not here — or to find it. That's the only way.'

After a lot of discussion Uncle Tom finally agreed to the sergeant's scheme, so that afternoon a van arrived at Jamaica Bay with a dozen policemen all dressed in light blue fatigues. Each one looked very serious, and Jim imagined that looking through an old man's house was pretty low down on a policeman's list of favourite things to do on a bright summer's afternoon.

Armed with chisels, hammers and screwdrivers, they all disappeared upstairs to the attic from where banging, shouting and the occasional laugh could be heard. Jim took Gemma for a walk.

'We've got a bit of a problem now, Gemma,' said Jim.

'They are bound to search the cellar,' Gemma replied. 'Do you think we ought to say something? I mean, we can't be certain there's going to be anything to find down there can we? But on the other hand, would we get into trouble if we didn't tell them there was something there?'

It was a prickly problem, which Jim pondered as they wandered slowly round the back of the house. He eventually said, 'Look, if we go down there on the pretext of playing a game or something and check what the police do, if they find it we can tell them all about it, but if they don't, well, we'll let things run. With all these policemen here I doubt very much whether Slater will show up. Not yet, anyway.'

So it was agreed that Gemma would take Pinky down to the cellar and sit on an upturned crate roughly where the trap door was. Jim, meanwhile, would go upstairs and stay with the search teams. If either one of them could put the police off discovering the trap door, then that is what they would do.

When Jim reached the first floor, the search team had already finished in one bedroom. Some were in Uncle Tom's room and some were in the other room. He could hear Uncle Tom causing a commotion because one of the policemen started fiddling with his instruments on "the bridge". Sergeant Mineards was doing his best to calm him down. The boy went into the other bedroom and sat on the unmade bed.

'Do you live here then?' one of the policemen asked.

'No' replied Jim, 'I'm only staying with my Uncle Tom whilst my mum is in hospital.'

The policeman stopped what he was doing and got onto all fours to search under the bed. He said, 'I'll bet you're bored stiff aren't you? There's not much for a small lad to do round here.'

'I'm really busy,' replied Jim. 'I'm really enjoying myself. I've even been out on the Cornish Pride at Pentilrock.'

The policeman gave a big smile. 'Well, it's a small world round here. Do you hear that, Ken — the boy here has been out with your Bob.'

'Your Bob?' asked Jim. 'Do you mean Bob Smith?'

'Yes,' replied P.C. Smith. 'Bob is my brother. I shall have to speak to him later and make sure you behaved yourself with him. See if I've got to look out for you in future.' He winked at his colleague Ken and gave a little chuckle.

'Now what on earth have we got here, then?' Ken announced in his best village policeman's voice. He was pulling a thick cord from under the bed. Gradually as he put more effort into his task, a large black mass of rubber appeared.

'What on earth is it?' asked the P.C. Smith. As they unravelled the folds and creases of the object Jim realised what it was.

'It's a rubber dinghy' he exclaimed.

'My goodness, your uncle keeps some things, doesn't he?' said P.C. Smith.

'I'll take that downstairs,' said Jim, only just managing to pick up the smelly rubber boat in his arms. He took it into the kitchen and threw it down in a heap.

'Where did you find that thing? Your uncle does keep some rubbish,' said Maureen.

'You are the second person to tell me that,' replied Jim with a smile.

'I thought Gemma and I could use it sometime, if we get a chance to get down to the sea.'

Maureen gave a frown and said, 'It looks as if it has seen better days. I doubt whether it has even felt water beneath it.'

Jim remembered Gemma, and leaving his new discovery in the kitchen, he went out and into the cellar. The police had already arrived there. Gemma had a worried look on her face.

'They've not found anything yet,' he told her. 'I doubt if they will down here either.'

'You never know your luck my lad,' said a friendly-looking policeman. All the shutters had been let down, allowing the cellar to be illuminated by the afternoon sunshine.

'Would you like me to sweep away that muck for you, officer?' asked Jim helpfully.

'Well you can I suppose. That's very kind of you,' replied the officer. Jim swept a small portion of the cellar floor at various places being careful not to interrupt the dirt near the trap door. The policemen banged the floor with hammers — if they happened to strike the trap door the game would be up. The policeman nearest Jim fiddled about with a chisel in the coal dust and then, as if finding a roll of £50 notes, cried 'Alan, what's this?'

He fumbled with his gloved fingers and began to pull on something. With a laugh he produced a black lump about half the size of his hand.

'Could this be the missing treasure that half of Devon and Cornwall Constabulary have been looking for? No, it's a piece of coal.' The other policemen, who had stopped what they where doing, laughed loudly at their friend's joke.

'Come on lads,' he said. 'We aren't going to find anything down here. Let's leave these kids in peace.'

They all climbed the wooden steps to the back yard where they patted down their clothes causing a cloud of dust to float across the ground like a fog.

'Tea up, lads,' called Maureen, as she produced a large tray carrying several mugs of tea along with a plate of biscuits. The policemen gathered round her like a football team getting their half-time oranges. Some of them sat on the ground drinking tea and talking, relaxing having completed their onerous task.

Feeling safe, Jim and Gemma pulled the shutters closed, leaving the feeble bulb to cast its ugly shadows. Jim told Gemma about his discovery under the bed upstairs.

'It could be very useful if we can get it down to the cave so we can do a proper search. It's handy the police have done what they have, because it certainly rules out finding the diamond anywhere else but down there.' He pointed to the ground.

'It's just a shame we are not going to have time to look today. I think Mum will call me to go soon. She was talking about having to do some errand tonight for old Mrs Jones further down the lane,' said Gemma, resigned to having to wait another day to take a further step down the unknown path of adventure.

The children decided to get the dinghy down into the cellar to save time the next day. Although he'd been warned, Jim did not imagine that the rubber craft would be damaged. Somehow he knew it would be okay. In a fashion that reminded the boy of his mother packing his bags to visit his uncle, the children had a line of items in the cellar, ready to take "below": torches, rubber dinghy, an old piece of rope, and a bag containing all sorts of useful things that Jim had previously jammed into his pockets.

As predicted, it wasn't long before Maureen called Gemma to go home. Time certainly had gone by quickly with all the activity at the house. The sun was already low in the sky when Uncle Tom and Jim sat down and ate their cold meat salad. Jim's great uncle seemed quite low in spirits, probably because finding The White Tiger was the only way of putting Slater off. The police had ended taking up the floor boards and unscrewing anything which could be removed. It would have been virtually impossible for the diamond to be at the house without the police finding it.

After dinner, the boy and his uncle sat on the veranda. The old man told Jim many tales of happier days back in Jamaica, when he was younger, of his sea faring days and his hopes for the future.

He puffed contentedly on his pipe making intriguing patterns in the cool evening air. Smoking his clay always seemed to put Uncle Tom in a good mood. Why, Jim couldn't imagine. Sucking the fumes into your lungs couldn't be that nice, even if it did smell sweet, particularly with all the warnings you see on cigarette adverts. No, Jim decided, he would stick with sucking sweets.

Immediately Jim thought of sweets, he jumped off the lounger and ran upstairs to the attic. From the bottom of one of the big wardrobes he pulled out the only bag he hadn't unpacked since his arrival.

Strangely, this one bag which he hadn't even thought about contained all the games and toys he had bought from home to keep himself amused. He rummaged through the books and boxes and eventually came across a large white paper bag. Throwing the packed bag back into the wardrobe he again rushed downstairs clutching his find to his chest.

He took his place again next to his great uncle and slowly opened the bag. Checking first to make sure he wasn't mistaken, he offered its contents to the old man.

'What's this then, Shrimp?' Uncle Tom peered inside. 'Coconut mushrooms,' he cried. 'I haven't had these since I was a lad. Fantastic!'

He popped one into his mouth and chewed on the morsel, making his beard twitch. The way he had reacted anyone would have though it had been a piece of perfectly cooked fillet steak. Both of them took another and then another. In fact neither of them stopped until the bag was empty and their chests were covered in coconut crumbs. It was a pleasant finish to a busy day.

Chapter 10

The next morning, Jim found his great uncle sitting at the kitchen table with a troubled expression on his face. He was surveying the morning's post, which was spread out in front of him.

'Morning, Uncle Tom,' said Jim cheerfully. 'Is everything okay?'

'Not bad, Shrimp. We've no Maureen today. She left a note saying she and Gemma have had to go away for a few days. Family trouble or something.'

He held a scrap of paper out for Jim to read. It said:

> *Tom, Sorry for the short notice, but note left for me when we returned home. My brother has trouble in Exeter. Had to leave straight away. Will ring in a few days if lines are working.*
>
> *Love,*
>
> *Maureen and Gemma.*

Jim looked up thoughtfully. His uncle was apparently untroubled by the note left overnight.

'Is that Maureen's normal writing?' he asked.

'That's a strange question,' said the old man, looking at the note. 'Yes, I'm sure it is.'

Uncle Tom gathered up all the papers and envelopes into a pile forcing them into a letter rack that stood on the worktop next to the back door. 'What are your plans for today, young Jim?'

'I think I'll just have a good look round, Uncle Tom. I haven't really had a chance yet,' said Jim.

'That's a good idea,' replied his great uncle. 'I've got some very important phone calls to make today. I'm afraid it's make or break time. My new financial advisor has been making some enquiries for me. I'll be around the house, so don't think twice about coming to me if you need anything.'

'I hope the phone's working,' joked Jim.

Uncle Tom went off to his study while Jim had his breakfast. It seemed strange not having Gemma and Maureen around. At least he would have the day free to sniff around and take the things down to the cave. He might even have time to search it at low tide.

Jim had also been giving a lot of thought to that other tunnel they had come across. As well as searching the cave, he needed to find out where the other passage led. He decided to have a walk along the cliffs and take some time looking at the beautiful surroundings. Gemma had talked to him about the pretty path from her house down to the cliffs, so Jim headed out along the weathered path from Jamaica Bay to Maureen and Gemma's cottage.

It was quite cloudy but warm. The huge trees rustled their leaves noisily, throwing the branches to and fro, making it impossible for any birds to rest. They sped across the sky playing on invisible waves of wind, showing off to each other.

The boy reached his friend's house. It looked deserted with the curtains in each room closed, like big eyelids over deep-set, tired eyes. The front gate was open, but he didn't go in. It seemed strange that they had to leave in the middle of the night without even a goodbye. Whatever was wrong with Gemma's uncle must be pretty serious. Strangely, the absence of the young girl made things seem different, as if a part was missing from a game or a puzzle. This surprised Jim, because he hadn't realised until now how much he liked Gemma and her mum.

A depressed mood hung over Jim now. He wandered along the cliffs, occasionally bending to pick up a stone before he hurled it over the edge. It was such a long way down he never actually saw one hit the water.

Just as he was thinking about heading back to his great uncle's house, Jim suddenly saw a man hurrying along the path towards him. The stranger was bent over against the strong breeze that blew in his face. He didn't see Jim until the two were almost on top of each other.

The man had dirty-coloured fair hair with a couple of days' growth on his chin. His sallow complexion made him look ill. A rather limp-looking home-made cigarette hung from his thin lips. His very worn black leather jacket was matched by a filthy pair of denim jeans, which in turn were finished off by a very thin-looking pair of pointed black shoes.

Jim stopped and watched him pass. The man scowled, forcing his hands deeper into his jacket pockets as he rushed past without saying anything. It struck the boy how out of place the stranger looked. He certainly wasn't taking the air or enjoying a leisurely stroll along the cliffs. He walked with a definite purpose. Jim wondered what that purpose was and where he was going.

Uncle Tom was still in his study when Jim got back to Jamaica Bay. He popped his head around the door and asked if there was anything he could do for the old man. Things weren't going too well by the looks of things. Jim didn't get a proper reply, only a grunt of recognition. He was best left to it.

Armed with his torch, Jim went into the cellar, switching on the dim light. The equipment revealed itself ready to be taken down to the cave. Would he be able to go back down by himself without Gemma? Thinking for a couple of minutes, the boy reached for the big hook in the floor. Using all his strength he managed to lift the awkward hatch to its upright position.

Things were very much as before. Jim hadn't expected any different. The dinghy was heavy but he managed to drag it to the place where the tunnel got very low, then putting it in front of him he used his feet to push the rubber boat along the passageway. It was a good thing the floor was smooth, thought Jim. His new-found boat would be worth very little with big rips and tears in it.

Eventually the passage opened up again into the cave. The sea sounded angry outside but was calm as a millpond within the enclosure of rock. Jim laid out the boat on the rocky platform. He found the large valve which was used to inflate it. Not having thought about it before, he closed his lips around the sour tasting ring and blew with all his might. For what seemed like ages, he continued blowing into the dinghy, until his head was spinning and stars danced before his eyes.

He fell back against the cave wall exhausted. The dinghy didn't look as if it had any air in it at all. Perhaps it did have some holes in it. Getting to his feet, Jim decided to go back to the cellar and get the rest of the things he and Gemma had got ready to bring down. When he returned to the cave, after struggling with the bag and rope, Jim set to and had another go at inflating the boat.

After several minutes of blowing, he looked at his charge with satisfaction. Funnily enough, once blown up, the cumbersome object seemed to be lighter. He easily pushed it from the platform into the water where it sat swaying gently. Using the frayed rope that was attached to the end of the boat, Jim tied it to the mooring ring fixed beneath the platform. The only things missing were the oars.

It was too late to have a good look around the cave in the dinghy so Jim decided to leave that until the next day. He didn't want to arouse Uncle Tom's suspicions by being missing for too long.

On the way back to the cellar, he stopped at the side of the tunnel and studied the wooden blockage. If only he could open it and discover where it went. Old Man Slater must have used these tunnels to slip out of the area or even out of the country unnoticed. There could be a whole maze of passages leading to who knows where. All in good time, he thought.

When Jim got back upstairs he found his uncle still sitting at his study desk. With his hat perched on the back of his head, he sat hunched over the papers with a large glass in one hand and a big bottle of Navy Rum in the other. He stared at nothing in particular on the table, with an expression the young boy had not seen before — a sadness so deep it seemed to make the old man shrink in size.

'What's wrong, Uncle Tom?' asked Jim. His uncle's sad face looked up from the papers with a glassy stare, and he shrugged his shoulders.

'Hello, Shrimp. Don't mind me — I'm only drowning my sorrows.'

'But what's wrong?' persisted the boy.

'Well, it's finally happened, that's all. It's very hard to explain everything, Jim, but in a nutshell, all the money I had was put into a small company that seemed to be doing well. "A sound investment" they told me. Well it wasn't. All my money, gone. Oh, I've got a little bit put by, but not enough to buy this place. I'm sorry Jim. I don't mean to burden your shoulders with my problems.'

Jim went around the desk and put a small arm round his uncle's neck.

'I don't know how,' he said, 'but somehow things are going to work out. Something will come up, you'll see.' A huge grin ran across his face as his uncle looked into his eyes.

'You wouldn't be taking one at me, would you, you young whippersnapper?' He laughed that deep gruff laugh of his, but Jim knew it wasn't a normal one. 'I'm sure you're right, Shrimp, something will come up'. The big man put the bottle in the bottom drawer of the desk and followed Jim out of the room.

Later that night, Jim lay in his hammock with Pinky on his chest. His little snout was very busy picking up all the interesting smells from his big friend. The little pink eyes appeared to squint at Jim, as he stroked the soft white fur.

He thought about his great uncle, who was probably standing on his "bridge" now, thinking about happier times. He wondered if he was going to be able to help in any way. Where would his uncle live? Would he go back to the West Indies? Whether he liked it or not, Jim had a feeling things would come to a head pretty soon.

The next day was pretty much like the ones before, except the wind and the cloud had relented, leaving a clear blue sky. Jim wasted no time. Thinking of the worst possible outcome, he slipped his swimming trunks on underneath his shorts and took a towel downstairs with him. Today was the day he would search the cave. The water was probably quite cold but it had to be done and, besides, he hadn't been swimming since he had arrived.

He ate his breakfast and spent quite a long time doing chores for his uncle: washing up, pegging washing on the line and sweeping the veranda. He even cleaned his uncle's Land Rover for him. The most satisfying job was to fetch the eggs from the chicken coup. It wasn't as bad as he expected and he brought back eight nice big eggs. Uncle Tom spent his morning in the study poring over papers and documents, but his mood had got brighter since the previous evening, as if he might have thought of a solution to his problems.

Once again armed with his torch, the brave young boy tied his towel around his neck and having opened his secret tunnel, he scrambled down onto the smooth rock and made his way, more quickly than before, to the large cave.

Much to his disappointment, the black dinghy, although still in the water, had gone down a little, making it look precarious as it wobbled constantly under the gentle movement of the clear water. He pulled the boat out of the water and re-inflated it. This did not take long, much to his relief. He then got the long piece of rope and tied it to the mooring ring that the dinghy was linked to. Very gently Jim eased himself onto the dinghy and untied it. Holding the long piece of rope he thrust the boat away from the side so that it floated across to the other side of the cavern.

Unfortunately, the water did have a little undercurrent, and the boat drifted away towards the furthest corner, some five metres from where he intended. He pulled at the rope and regained his position at the platform. He repeated the process twice more before he got to where he wanted to be.

He threaded the rope through the other mooring ring, which lay opposite the rock outcrop, and pulled it tight. Using the now taut line Jim pulled himself back to his original position, rethreading the rope through the ring. He tied a knot, still leaving several metres loose trailing like a long snake in the water.

The young boy stripped off down to his swimming trunks and stood on the rock, thinking. He didn't even know exactly what he was going to do. He hadn't really considered it before this moment, but he was sure that he ought to search below the waterline in case anything was hidden there.

Stepping once more into the dinghy, Jim picked up the loose piece of rope and holding on to it tightly slipped quickly over the side into the sea. His breath was immediately taken from him leaving him gasping and gulping like a 400 metre runner who hadn't trained. He let his body adjust to the temperature and then tentatively started out towards the back of the enclosure, feeling his way like a mime artist along the wall of the cave below the water line. Jim made sure he hung on to the rope just in case he was taken by surprise. He felt the strong undertow of the invisible current plucking at his body, even at the sides. It must be far worse in the middle, he thought.

The cave was too deep for Jim to touch the bottom but he continued as best he could around the edge for what seemed like ages. His fingers became prune-like and his heart jumped every time his hands laid upon a piece of slippery seaweed or slimy rock that moved under his grip.

At the very back of the cave, some six metres from the platform, Jim realised the rope was stretched as far as it would go. Just as he thought to himself he would have to be careful, a swell lifted him up, taking the rope from his grasp. He clung to the rocks with his back to the cave, knowing that if he slipped, the ebbing tide would drag him from his perch and suck him through the filter of craggy rocks, cutting his fragile body to ribbons. His closest safety point was the rope tied to the mooring ring opposite the platform. If he could only reach there everything would be fine. Very slowly, Jim felt his way along the smooth walls, looking for any small handhold to steady himself. Each gentle swell lifted him effortlessly like an empty bottle, making it almost impossible to hold on. Slowly, slowly he edged closer to the taut rope stretched across the cave. His feet scraped slimy rocks and anchored limpets as he drew nearer.

Suddenly a large swell lifted him much higher than any before it. Jim lost his grip and started to struggle. As the mass of water started to roller-coaster down, it sent him pitching towards the rope. With one hand he stretched up as the other grazed the rock wall. He was too low — he was slipping underneath it. Then his other hand came into contact with something below the water. He grabbed it, turning himself in the water so that he could use both hands. He hung on to it as if his life depended on it, as indeed it did. The water fell to its normal level and Jim found himself hanging onto an old chain that was forced into the wall just below the mooring ring.

For a few minutes he hung there, lifeless, gradually feeling his body start to tremble all over. That was close. He had totally lost control of the situation, and he didn't like it. He must get out to feel solid ground beneath his feet again.

He reached up and felt the thick rope above his head. He was safe. Nothing else mattered. Perhaps he could have a better look round when Gemma came back.

The cold young boy was about to let go of his underwater hold when a thought struck him.

Why was there a chain in the water below a mooring ring? He pulled it. It was heavy but free. He pulled and pulled. The thick linked chain gradually came into view, but it was cumbersome and too heavy for him.

Letting go, he scooted across the rope to the platform and hoisted himself out of the water. He untied the dinghy and retied it to the rope across the cave. Then, with excitement coursing through his body, he jumped back into the dinghy and pulled it across to the opposite side. Being above the water, he now had a much better position from which to haul in the old chain. A few links at a time, the great metal rope was hoisted aboard. There must have been six or seven metres of it, so much in fact that Jim thought it might capsize his boat if he hauled up any more.

Suddenly the chain stopped coming, and a large greasy looking bag appeared over the side. Jim threw it in the bottom of the dinghy, and sat back quickly as if it contained poisonous snakes or a contagious disease.

He pulled himself back to the platform and hurriedly unloaded the chain onto the rock floor, allowing it to stretch across the cave like the rope. The small boy towelled himself off, hardly daring to speculate about what he had found. He didn't take his eyes off the canvas bag at his feet.

It was a square-shaped, sack-like container with holes along its top, through which a length of wire had been threaded. This in turn was attached to the heavy chain. One thing was certain, this bag had been left on the end of the chain intentionally, in a place where it was unlikely to be found.

As Jim tried to untwist the wire from the chain, it snapped, leaving the bag free. He was now shaking, not through the cold but from sheer excitement. He may well be on the edge of another step in his adventure.

Chapter 11

Still shaking, Jim again tried to unthread the wire, and once again it snapped, leaving the bag's opening to fall apart. Jim gently held the bottom of it, and tipped the contents onto the floor. Out fell a very heavy iron bar, about 20 centimetres long, and another object.

The second item was about the size of a tennis ball and also quite heavy, and wrapped in muslin. Jim started to unwind the cloth. He took a sharp breath, for in his hand was the most fascinating sight he had ever seen. Although it was quite dim in the cave, the colours that seemed to emanate from the glass ball in his hand lit up his face as he gave a huge Yippee! — for he was looking at The White Tiger, the one diamond that had been missing for all these years. James George Wills had found it!

He quickly dressed, tugging his T-shirt over his damp back, and his socks and trainers onto his wet feet. He didn't care. All he felt was elation.

He suddenly stopped. What should he do now? What should he do with the diamond? Should he hide it or tell his great uncle, or … who knows? Slater was still at large and he may still come looking for it. As Gemma had said, it was doubtful he knew about the cave because surely that would be the obvious place to look. He decided. He would hide the diamond temporarily, and take a walk to Gemma's to see If she was back yet. If she was not there he would have to tell Uncle Tom.

Leaving the iron bar on the platform, he threw the chain back into the water. He then deposited the diamond back in the bag and with his towel tied around his neck made his uncomfortable way back to the cellar.

He replaced the hatch door and carefully re-covered it with dirt. Jim knew exactly where he would hide his find. Having successfully secreted his treasure, he found his uncle asleep across his desk. He obviously hadn't slept very well the night before, due to his money worries.

Jim whispered, 'Never mind, Uncle. Something will come up, you'll see.'

He quietly left the house and made his way along the path. Jim didn't know how to contain his excitement, but Gemma would be pleased with his work.

It was a hot afternoon, and Jim felt as happy as he could ever remember. Nothing exciting had ever happened to him before, but now he had found one of the best known diamonds in the world, and possibly solved his uncle's financial problems — that is, if a reward was still being offered for the return of The White Tiger to Holland.

He skipped along through the wood until Gemma's cottage came into view. It was drenched in sunlight and looked very picturesque. Suddenly he stopped. The curtains of the house were open, as was one of the windows, so Gemma and Maureen must be back already and they hadn't had time to come down to Jamaica Bay. He started off again but almost immediately stopped. Walking from the direction of the cliffs, bent over as if struggling against a strong wind, and still wearing scruffy jeans and his worn leather jacket, was the man Jim had seen on the cliffs the day before.

To the boy's amazement, the scruffy man turned into Gemma's garden. He stopped and knocked heavily on the door. After a few seconds the door opened and the man passed inside. Jim froze and felt like his heart had stopped beating as another man came out of the house, looked to the left and to the right in a furtive manner and then went back inside, closing the door. The young boy's head pounded as the gravity of the situation dawned on him. There was no mistake. The man that emerged from the house was definitely Slater.

That could mean only one of two things; either Slater and his friend had broken in after Maureen and Gemma had left for Exeter — or Slater was holding Maureen and Gemma hostage until he could make Uncle Tom move. Jim's thoughts were now racing.

Could there be more than two of them? Was there anyone watching Uncle Tom's house? Were Maureen and Gemma in the cottage or not? He had to think quickly. What on earth should he do?

Chapter 12

Jim assumed a position adjacent to the path but under cover of the dense foliage of bushes and heathers. It took time for his brain to decide upon his first step — he should get as close as he could to the open window and see if he could hear anything from inside.

Jim was about forty metres from the front gate. He could not approach the cottage directly, which meant fighting his way through the greenery in front of the house so that he could get into the garden on the cliff side of the cottage, thereby remaining unseen. After only ten minutes, Jim was wishing he had a pair of trousers on and not shorts. The thick vegetation scratched his legs and pulled at his clothes, tearing holes in the thin fabric. He almost cried out on a couple of occasions as pain seared through his limbs and torso.

Eventually he emerged onto the cliff path. He was covered in grazes and was breathing heavily. He crossed over and forced his way through a few more bushes until he found himself in the garden next to the old well. Silently and with great caution, he edged up to the wall of the cottage, as he had seen so many people do on the television. He flattened himself against the wall, and pushed himself round until his head was next to the open window.

A lamp was on inside, and even in the late afternoon sun he could see a very good reflection of the room in the glass of the open window, which faced him. Fortunately, the heavy thatch hung down, casting shadows over the walls. Again Jim stopped breathing as he made out the image of Maureen sitting in a chair next to the lamp.

'You can't keep us here for ever,' he heard Maureen say.

'Shut up. I don't need you to tell me what I can or can't do. I don't think you are in any position to give me advice, do you?'

It was Slater's voice. Jim would always remember that harsh tone.

The voice continued, 'It won't hurt to let you know anyway. Everything depends on how your old mate up the lane behaves. If he won't get out then I need time to look for what is rightfully mine.'

'Rightfully yours?' That was Gemma's voice. 'There is nothing here that belongs to you. Poor Uncle Tom. You have got no right to … '

'No right? Shut up! How can I expect one so young to understand the intricacies of the situation? My father worked hard to get where he got to and he left something here, my rightful inheritance.' Slater was getting cross.

Gemma went on. 'The White Tiger is not yours.'

There was a long silence before Slater could be heard moving across the room. Gemma screamed a shrill cry,

124

and Jim moved to the edge of the window where he could just see inside.

'The White Tiger? Who the hell said anything about the White Tiger? Tell me what you know about it.'

There was silence.

'Tell me!' shouted Slater. He shook Gemma by the shoulders. 'Tell me what you know.'

Maureen shouted at Slater, 'Leave her alone. She knows nothing. Nor do I. None of us do.'

'Liars!' shouted Slater.

'We are not lying,' sobbed Maureen. 'Tom told us all about your father. I assume your name is Slater. He told us that when your father was arrested all the diamonds from the Amsterdam robbery were found, except the biggest, The White Tiger. Tom assumed that the only reason you were causing trouble with him now was the fact that you are looking for the diamond.'

'He is assuming an awful lot,' hissed Slater. He threw Gemma back into a chair.

'Well I am going to find it,' he continued. 'It's worth millions, even after it has been divided up. Naturally, I couldn't sell it in its present form. It would be recognised too easily.'

'Well Uncle Tom doesn't know where it is. Even the police couldn't find it,' said Gemma.

'The police,' sneered Slater. 'The police are useless. They wouldn't know the first place to start looking.'

Gemma went on with an arrogant edge to her voice. 'Well they are going to find you very soon and put you in the same place as your father, prison.'

Slater moved very close to Gemma so that his face was almost touching hers. 'The thing is, little girl, Mr Policeman will know that you and your mumsy-wumsy have gone to Exeter, and they won't come looking here for me will they? Oh no. You see I'll be so frightened, I've probably gone to London or Manchester while things quieten down. I wonder if you and your mum will ever be found? Do you know what I mean?'

He gave a high-pitched laugh that pierced the air and sounded evil, somehow out of place in the peaceful setting. Silence invaded the menacing scene, and Jim shrank back from the window slightly, allowing himself to breathe normally for the first time.

'Lenny,' Slater said, 'shut that window and come outside. It is time for a talk.'

The window banged shut, and Jim started to panic. He was about to be discovered.

Quick as a flash, he ran to the well and clambered over the low wall. As the door of the cottage opened, the boy lowered himself into the dark recess, until his foot found a hole to slip into. Amazingly, the cement holding the bricks together four rows down was missing, allowing Jim to wedge his fingers in and cling on.

'I don't like this, Slater,' a voice said. 'How long have we got to hold onto this pair for?'

'Stop complaining,' said Slater. 'They are our insurance should anything go wrong. Not that I am expecting anything to go wrong, Lenny. If it does, it is bound to be your fault.'

The man Lenny interrupted. 'That's not fair, Slater. I couldn't avoid being seen by the boy. Anyway, he probably thought I was out for a stroll.'

'No matter!' snapped Slater. 'By tomorrow evening our friends will arrive and we'll finish the job, and very glad I will be too. Get into the kitchen and cook some grub. I'm feeling peckish.'

Lenny muttered something and went back into the cottage. Jim was just about to climb back out of the well when Slater appeared above him. Once again Jim froze. Slater turned his back and sat on the wall. He fumbled in front of him and then Jim heard a match being struck. The rogue lit a cigarette and then tossed the match down the well, causing Jim to stifle a yelp as the hot splinter fell on his bare arm. Slater stood up and turned around. The boy was petrified. He tried to lower himself slightly more, feeling for a foothold with his spare foot. Incredibly, he felt a protrusion from the wall and silently settled down onto it loosening his handhold. Still frightened at the prospect of Slater discovering him, Jim settled even lower, taking his foot out of its original hole. There beneath his other foot he found another foothold. This time as he lowered himself he was able to put his hand in the first foot hole.

Lower and lower Jim slipped, deftly manoeuvring himself out of sight of the top of the well head. Slater disappeared but then suddenly leant right over the well head. Jim looked up and for a moment thought he had been discovered, but then Slater whispered, 'A penny a wish.' He threw a coin down the hole, hitting the boy on the head. It bounced and then fell to the bottom with a clink.

'I wish for tremendous wealth and no problems,' said the man. He gave a chuckle and again disappeared from Jim's view.

Jim found himself in two minds. He knew he had to help Gemma and Maureen, but something told him he should keep climbing down. He was already over half way, he decided, so why not continue?

To his relief he found some metal steps had been cemented into the wall at regular intervals. They enabled both a foot to rest upon them and a hand to grip them, as one might hold the rungs of a ladder. Jim's initial thought was that these were to enable an inspection of the well for maintenance purposes. Once at the bottom, the boy had trouble standing up because of rocks and pebbles which had obviously been thrown down over the years. He looked up at the small circle of light, high above him. The bottom was completely dry but smelled very damp with a musty tang, as if water did pass here occasionally.

The light breeze ruffled Jim's hair as he stood there wondering what to do next. There was sometimes a familiar smell in the air, particularly when the breeze blew strongly. Something wasn't quite right. Whoever heard of a breeze at the bottom of a well? Jim shuffled his feet so that he stood on solid ground. Then, using the instep of his foot, he kicked a stone. It cracked loudly on the side of the well and rebounded, striking him just below his knee. He bit his bottom lip until he tasted blood. The last thing he needed now was for Slater to find him. Carefully he repeated his effort to kick a stone away, this time in the opposite direction. To the boy's utter astonishment, the stone rolled and clattered as it travelled away from him. It must be another passageway! From the distance it travelled, he could only assume that the tunnel he had found went downhill slightly. He knelt down, feeling with his hands like a blind man.

The passage was about three and a half feet high, and probably the same in width. Its sides were angular and rough, not smooth. If Jim's calculations were correct, he had found the other end of the blocked-off tunnel. The direction was certainly about right. If only he had had a torch with him he could go further. He could even get back to his uncle's house undetected. As it was he would have to do his best to get back to the top of the well, get out of the garden and retrace his steps though the undergrowth. His only chance of helping Gemma and her mum was to remain undetected. He started to ascend the sheer wall of the well, and it was only then that tiredness began to take its toll on him. After all, he had done an awful lot today and he wasn't finished yet. Any joy he felt at finding the diamond had been replaced by concern and fear.

Once at the top, he peered over the edge. The coast was clear, the garden was empty. He clambered out and managed to squeeze through the bushes and thorny undergrowth, out across the path and back through the natural assault course again, tearing his clothes and scratching his bare arms and legs. Some thirty minutes later he had made it. Half-stumbling, half-running, he made his way back along the path to Jamaica Bay. How much was he to tell his uncle? Would Uncle Tom be cross with him? Only one way to find out, he thought.

When he got back Uncle Tom was in the kitchen making tea. He took one look at his nephew and said, 'My goodness. Look, at the state of you and the price of fish, my lad. What have you been doing?'

'It's Maureen and Gemma, Uncle. They are in great danger. Slater, it's Slater!' Words tumbled from him as though someone had turned a tap on.

'Hold on, Shrimp, hold on. Sit down. Take your time. What is this you are saying? Gemma and Maureen? But they are in Exeter. You saw the note, lad.'

'No, no!' shouted Jim. 'They are at home, I've been there. Slater and a man called Lenny have got them tied up in the cottage. I've been there, Uncle. I've listened to them talking.'

Uncle Tom sat at the kitchen table, as Jim carried on telling him what he had seen. His mouth dropped further and further open, until Jim had finished. The old man moved his straw hat and scratched his head. What he had just heard was utterly fantastic, but knowing even a little of Slater, he knew it was probably the truth.

'Well that's a turn-up. You should have come back for me. It's too dangerous, Jim. You are only a boy,' said Uncle Tom.

'But Uncle,' explained Jim, 'only I could have done it. I hid down the well. If you had been there we would have been caught. As it is, Slater and his mate don't know that we know that they are there.'

'Yes, you're probably right,' replied the old sailor. 'Before we do anything, I think we need to go there so that I can see for myself. It's one thing you telling me, Jim, but Sergeant Mineards is more likely to act if I can tell him that I have seen Slater and his oppo. First things first, though, my lad — let's get you cleaned up and have a bite to eat.'

Jim realised he had eaten nothing since breakfast and he was famished. He also told his uncle about Slater's plan to finish the job by tomorrow evening. An hour later, Jim and his uncle were ready to investigate the occupants of Maureen's cottage.

'We don't want to take a torch with us, Jim. We will not be able to use it.' It was dusk, and getting darker rapidly, but Jim had no intention of using it in the open.

'When we get there, Uncle, I'll explain why I've got the torch, and also these.' Jim lifted his sweatshirt to reveal a belt a hammer and an old screwdriver.

'Now, Jim, what are you up to?' asked the old man.

'Uncle, I hope you trust me. I'd rather explain when we get there,' said Jim.

'Okay Jim,' his uncle replied, 'but I'll not be letting you do anything dangerous.'

Jim smiled. He wondered what the old man would have said if he had told him that he had nearly drowned in a secret cave under the house whilst recovering The White Tiger earlier today.

'What are you laughing at lad?' asked Uncle Tom.

'Oh nothing, Uncle Tom. Nothing.' What would the night bring, he wondered.

Jim and his uncle silently made their way along the path towards the small cottage. A gentle wind rustled the trees, their leaves passing secret messages to each other. In only a few minutes the two ill-matched figures came to rest a little way from the house.

'There — look Uncle. In the right-hand room. The light is on,' pointed out Jim.

'That doesn't mean that Slater is there,' said Uncle Tom. 'It might just be Maureen is home but hasn't had time to come and see us.'

As if on cue, the front door opened and Lenny stepped out, followed by Slater.

'Well, I don't think it is necessary, Slater. They will not give us any trouble tomorrow,' said Lenny, as his faced glowed in the light of his cigarette.

'When will you just do as I ask, Lenny? We need to have a rough idea of who is there. If the old man has the local coppers visiting him on a regular basis I would like to know as much as I can. Come back in a couple of hours after they have gone to bed. Now get out of here.' The man Lenny walked miserably away off towards the cliffs, as Slater took a deep breath and stretched his arms.

'Well, Jim, you are quite right lad. Looks like Maureen and Gemma are in real danger,' murmured Uncle Tom.

Jim looked at the old man's face. 'Uncle, I know it's difficult to believe, but I may be able to help them.'

'Oh Jim. You do go on. Go on then, tell me.'

'I don't mean now, but I need to check something out. Will you go home and wait for me ... in the cellar?'

'In the cellar?' blustered his Uncle. 'In the cellar? What on earth do you mean, Shrimp?'

'I told you I hid in the well this afternoon. Well I'm going to go down it again now.'

'But why?' asked Uncle Tom.

'As I said, you'll have to trust me. I promise I will tell you later. Wait here until I have actually got inside, and then go back. I'll be about half an hour before I'll be with you.'

'But why the cellar?' asked Uncle Tom.

'Trust me,' answered Jim.

'Okay, Shrimp,' said the old man rubbing the top of the boy's head, 'but any sign of danger, and I'll be over there like a flash. Be careful.'

With a thumbs-up, Jim quietly slipped into the darkness, heading towards the small cottage. The old sailor squinted in an effort to see the house and its garden more clearly. He was just able to make out his small nephew push his way into some bushes and seconds later appear next to the old well. With a small move Jim disappeared down the hole. Uncle Tom was worried, but the young boy had a good head on his shoulders. Tom thrust his hands into his old boiler-suit pockets, and wandered off slowly back to Jamaica Bay.

As he walked, he thought about the sudden developments surrounding his very existence at Jamaica Bay. So Slater was having the house watched. He must be deadly serious about getting his hands on the stolen diamond, but where could it be hidden? Having taken

Maureen and Gemma, there was a lot more at stake than just an old piece of rock that happened to be worth a fortune. He would have to have a think, sitting in the cellar of all places.

Meanwhile, Jim had reached the bottom of the well. It was quite daunting searching a passage he hadn't been in before. What was he going to find? Being very careful not to shine his torch up the well or onto the walls he looked down the tunnel. Because it was roughly made it seemed to vary in shape and size on every side.

He managed to negotiate the opening standing up, but bent over slightly. One thing he was grateful for was that the height of it was consistent. He made very good progress. The angular pieces of rock jutting out from the sides cast weird shadows, reminding Jim of the times he had sat with his parents watching an open coal fire with the light off, shadows dancing all around them as if they were in a haunted wood.

That same familiar smell reached him, the same one that he and Gemma had smelt when they had lifted the trap door for the first time. Suddenly, in front of him lay the large wooden blockage he had seen in the tunnel leading to the cave. He had travelled about fifty metres from the well, downhill most of the way. The barrier looked as if Jim had guessed correctly in that it was formed from the top of a barrel. Wooden blocks had been wedged around the circle making it a solid obstruction.

Jim rested his torch on the floor where it still cast a light on the barrier. Taking the hammer and screwdriver from his belt, he set about removing the wood from the tunnel. Some of the blocks came out very easily, whilst others Jim had to hit with great force to remove them, while trying not to make too much noise.

Eventually all the blocks were removed, and the round wooden wall fell inwards towards Jim. He caught it and leaned it up against the wall. He had done it. Lying in front of him was the other tunnel, which Jim scampered into having recovered his torch.

Uncle Tom sat on an upturned crate, leaning against his old workbench. He had returned home and been waiting in the cellar for about ten minutes. His time was occupied with making patterns with an old pencil in the dirt which had built up over the years. He didn't even know what half of the things around him were. He had spent virtually no time in here at all. His mind was grappling with the problems of the situation which surrounded him and his young nephew, when suddenly he heard a strange noise. A noise that he didn't recognise. He stopped what he was doing and listened intently. He could still hear it but couldn't quite place where it was coming from.

Suddenly the ground before him erupted, sending clouds of coal dust and dirt into the air, with the dim electric light bulb not giving out too much light the filthy atmosphere made it seem like an eclipse. Uncle Tom staggered to his feet, amazed at the sight before him. His little nephew stood in a hole with a large wooden trap door leant against the cellar wall behind him.

'Bless my barnacles,' gasped Uncle Tom. 'What have you found, boy? How did you know? When did you find it?' Questions poured out at the young boy who stood below him, laughing.

The old man could only look at his nephew with open admiration and awe as he briefly told him his tale — leaving out the bit about finding the diamond.

'Bless my soul,' said Uncle Tom. 'No wonder you and Gemma have spent so much time down here.'

Jim got out of the tunnel and shut the trap door, covering it with the dirt. Together they went into the house laughing, unaware that Lenny was sitting just behind the chicken coop.

How much had he seen and heard?

Chapter 13

Jim and his great uncle talked long into the night. One thing that they were both sure of was Slater's unpredictability. He may stop at nothing to get what he wanted — and that included hurting Maureen and Gemma. Over a cup of hot chocolate it was finally decided. Whilst involving the police might push Slater into doing something horrible to their friends, they could probably count on the help of Frank and the Cornish Pride. The one big thing which might help them was the secret tunnels leading to the cave and the open sea. It was obvious now that Slater knew nothing of their existence.

'At the end of the day,' mused Uncle Tom, 'the only thing that matters is the safety of those girls. Once we have got them safe, Slater and his gang can do what they like to the house. I won't be staying here and it is very doubtful they will find what they want. When we know that no harm will come to the girls, then we can let Sergeant Mineards know. What do you say, Shrimp?'

Jim agreed completely with the old man. They eventually went upstairs where the young boy was very grateful to lie down and shut his eyes. Sleep came to him easily, as it had done to Lenny who was lying amongst the undergrowth at the back of the house, completely oblivious to the plans of Jim and his uncle. It was three o'clock in the morning before he awoke and stiffly staggered back to the cottage where he got a very cool reception from his boss.

Early the next morning, Jim was woken up by his uncle and went downstairs to see a full breakfast laid out ready for him.

'If we are having an adventure today, I think we will do it on a full stomach, eh boy?' joked the old sailor.

Jim really enjoyed the eggs and bacon followed by toast and marmalade. It seemed to set him up for the day. Without bothering to tidy up the dishes, they both jumped into the Land Rover and set out for Pentilrock and the Cornish Pride, where Frank and his crew would be getting the boat ready for the day's fishing trip. Little did the fishermen know that it would end in excitement.

It didn't take long to reach the small harbour, where the working day was already well under way. Frank was very surprised to see the old man and his nephew so early in the day.

'Well, what brings you two out so early? We've got nothing for you yet I'm afraid.' He saw the unusual expression on Tom's face and beckoned them to come aboard. He led them to the wheelhouse where they told him the terrible tale.

'But that's awful, Tom. Are you sure they've got them?' he asked.

'I actually saw them tied up in the house,' confirmed Jim. 'Slater got very angry with Gemma because she mentioned The White Tiger diamond. He was furious. I thought he was going to hit her, but he didn't.'

'How can I help?' asked Frank.

Uncle Tom told the burly fisherman exactly what they thought about telling the police and about their plan to rescue the girls.

'At the slightest sign of trouble we will get Colin Mineards and all his crew in,' said the old man. 'But otherwise I think it's too risky. Slater has more men arriving this afternoon and then I think they will pay a little visit to Jamaica Bay. The only hope is for Jim to somehow lead Maureen and Gemma down the tunnel to a waiting boat. It would be too dangerous to come back to my place.'

'What time do you want me there?' asked Frank.

'Three o'clock should do it,' said Uncle Tom. And so it was agreed. The plan was laid and a rescue attempt was to be made.

All this made very interesting listening for the figure who was busy near to the door of the wheelhouse. Bob Smith had heard every word that was said and gave a very satisfied nod as he finished his task and left the boat, making an easy excuse to one of the others on board. Someone he knew would be happy to hear his news.

The Land Rover made its way back to Jamaica Bay, its occupants remaining silent for the entire journey. It was another fine day; just lately they had almost come to expect the sunshine every day. It seemed that this place in Cornwall would never again see wintry weather, like some tropical island dropped there by accident.

Once back at the house Jim and his great uncle went into the kitchen. The old man turned to his nephew and said, 'Are you sure you want to go through with this, Jim? It's an awful lot to ask of a young chap like you. It's no disgrace to say you won't do it, you know. I'm sure the police could find a way of sorting the mess out.'

Jim looked at his uncle, and suddenly felt quite grown up. Somebody was actually asking his opinion about things. He would be the one to help Maureen and Gemma. Nobody else, just him. He puffed his chest out like a courting pigeon and said, 'No, Uncle Tom. Only I know the cave and its passages. It's up to me.'

'I don't suppose you fancy showing your old Uncle Tom this cave, do you? I would quite like to see where all the action is going to take place.'

Jim liked that idea, and together the two of them left the kitchen and went into the cellar. After a few minutes the trap door was attached to the chain on the wall and the boy and his uncle had disappeared. Where the tunnel narrowed Uncle Tom had a little difficulty squeezing through: the years told their story as they gathered around his midriff, a constant reminder of his good living in the West Indies.

142

Jim stopped at the point where the two tunnels met, and explained how he had had to remove the wooden blockage that had been wedged there. If the old sailor was impressed by the tunnels his amazement at the sight that awaited him in the cave was a pleasure to watch.

'By Jingo, Jim. You've really found a little hideaway here, haven't you?' he exclaimed. He took his time looking round the cave then he noticed the iron bar lying on the stony platform.

'What's this you've found?' Jim was at a loss initially to explain how he came by it. He still didn't want to tell his uncle about his find.

'Oh I found it lying where it is. I don't know what it might have been used for. Do you recognise your boat?' he asked. He thought the change of subject was very skilful.

'Yes, I was keeping that for a rainy day. I was sure it would come in handy sometime,' Uncle Tom answered.

'Well you are certainly right there,' said Jim. 'Unfortunately it has a slow leak.'

Once again the dinghy rippled all along its sides in time with the moving water beneath it. Jim pulled the boat partially out of the water onto the platform and the old man bent over and with a couple of large breaths, filled the rubber dinghy until it looked solid. Apparently satisfied, Jim pushed it back into the sea.

'I've got some oars upstairs for it, Jim. You'll have to bring those down before you go for Maureen and Gemma.'

Having seen enough, the two of them retraced their steps back to the cellar where they again covered up the trap door. It was as well to be on the safe side, in case Slater or any of his men came sniffing round early.

It was almost time to act, and the butterflies Jim felt in his stomach were the size of blackbirds. He had never been so nervous about anything before in his whole life. Under the watchful eye of his great uncle he had gathered together a few things he thought might come in useful. The old man had also given him a very sharp knife, which had its own sheath that looped around his belt. He also had a length of strong twine, which he had curled up and put in his pocket. The other thing his uncle had given him, which was a surprise, was another pouch which fitted onto his belt: inside was a long ship's flare. The distress flare could be used to get help quickly if Jim found himself marooned on the cliffs — or out at sea if Frank didn't make it in time. To Jim's surprise, his uncle went to the back door in the kitchen and started fiddling with the large food cupboard fixed to the wall immediately behind it. Using his great bulk he pushed his big arm down one side of it, and pushed. Gradually, the big wardrobe-sized piece of furniture slid noisily to one side revealing a small door approximately two feet square and secured by a bolt. He undid the bolt and pushed the door: it moved to and fro as a cat flap might.

'This must have been used as a laundry chute or something years ago,' he said. 'You may as well use this instead of the back door in case any unwanted eyes are looking out for things.'

Jim had often wondered what the slide-shaped channel in the cellar wall was used for. Now he knew. He looked at his uncle who walked up to him and gave him a big hug.

'You make me very proud, lad,' said his uncle. 'If anything looks dodgy you come straight back or let off your flare.'

'Okay,' replied Jim.

'I'll be waiting where we were last night, just in case something goes wrong. Have you got that other torch?'

Jim showed him the two torches he was taking with him. He was ready. Without waiting he stuck one leg through the hatch and waved to his great uncle. The door flapped as he disappeared like a large feline creature. His great uncle drew a heavy sigh and, picking up another flare he had left on the table, he walked out of the front door.

It had been decided that Jim should leave quite early in case an opportunity to get the girls arose. In all probability there would be only one chance, and the boy had to take it. The old man went as quietly and as inconspicuously as he could, settling himself down in a large patch of heather and ferns. It may be a long wait but there was no alternative. Meanwhile, Jim made the journey down to the cave with the retractable oars his uncle had found for him. The dinghy was all ready. He made sure there was only a loose knot securing the craft to the mooring ring. There was no telling how quickly they may have to move on the way back.

He steadily progressed back up the tunnel, and then turned right towards the well and the two captives who were the centre of all his thoughts. Once at the foot of the well he rested a while, leaving the torches on the floor where they could be picked up easily on the return journey. He took hold of the first metal rung; his head was pounding and his heart pushed against his rib cage. From here it was the point of no return. Nobody could help him now.

With renewed effort, he climbed the well, pausing as his head emerged from the top. The sun still shone in a clear blue sky making him squint in the harsh glare. It was quite painful after the complete darkness of the tunnels. His body lifted slightly as he tried to get a view of what was happening at the cottage. He could just see the front face of the cottage from his position. The window of the room nearest to him was once again open and he could hear voices from inside, although it was impossible to make out what was being said or who was saying it.

Jim was just going to hoist himself out of the well when he saw Slater emerge from the cottage. He was drawing heavily on a cigarette, whilst resting his hands on his hips. He checked his watch and was obviously waiting for someone or something. He began to pace up and down, then suddenly he turned towards the cliff path and yelled, 'Where the hell do you think you've been? You're half an hour late, you fool. I knew I should have got someone else. You are useless. Now wait here and don't foul it up or you will live to regret it.'

A very dejected looking Lenny came into Jim's view. It was fairly obvious he had been asleep by the looks of him. Jim thought looked terrible.

Slater disappeared round the far end of the cottage and emerged with a very ancient looking bicycle. He pointed a finger at Lenny and said, 'I'm warning you. If anything goes wrong, I'll hold you personally responsible. This is our only chance, Lenny, so let's get it right.'

Lenny made a rude sign behind his master's back as Slater rode off towards Pentilrock, along the narrow weather-beaten path. With a laugh, Lenny went into the house. Jim now felt it was safe to climb out of the well and assume the same position he had held the day before, against the wall next to the window. He listened carefully.

'Well, it'll soon be over for you, my lovelies.' It was Lenny. 'Just as soon as my mate meets up with some associates, they'll be able to get on and find the stash. As soon as that's done, we'll be gone, unless something goes wrong, of course.' He gave a low, throaty laugh.

Jim pushed himself forward slightly so that he could see into the room. Lenny was sitting with his back to Jim. In his grubby hands the boy could see that he was toying with a lethal looking handgun, its dark metal shining in the shaded sunlight in the room. The young boy shrank back from the window, his mind racing with this new and unexpected development.

From his hiding place, Uncle Tom rubbed his chin thoughtfully as he surveyed the scene. He could see his little nephew apparently resting near the window of the room where they expected the girls to be held. He'd seen Slater ride off on the bicycle.

Were there only two of them or had Slater's mates arrived? He would stick to the plan and remain hidden. He was safe enough where he was.

If the old man thought he was unseen then he was wrong, for only six metres from him lay another dark and sinister stranger. The man watching both Uncle Tom and Jim was a very fit and athletic looking person wearing a green pullover and camouflaged trousers. He was obviously well used to making do, observing things. He wore a pair of binoculars around his neck and kept a small rucksack near to him. Unless something went terribly wrong he would remain hidden. It was all part of the plan.

Conversation had stopped in the cottage, and once again Jim edged forward and looked into the room. Lenny was still sitting in the same chair, only now he was leaning back holding his gun over his chest. It wasn't long before snoring could be heard. After all, no one would be stupid enough to tackle a man with a gun even if he was asleep.

Gaining confidence, Jim pushed his head further forward. He now had a complete view of the room. Gemma lay on a sofa resting, and Maureen sat in a chair near the lamp. Upon seeing Jim she sat bolt upright. He held a finger up to his lips. Now Gemma noticed Jim too. The feeling of relief must have been great for the mother and her daughter knowing that at last someone knew of their plight, and might raise the alarm. If they knew what plan Jim actually had they wouldn't have been so happy.

The boy gestured to Gemma and her mother to stay where they were. He left the window and sat behind the wall. Should he chance his luck and try to get in and out with Lenny asleep, or should he wait? How long was Slater going to be? He looked at his watch; two o'clock. Things could get difficult.

Slater was sweating badly as he got off the bicycle and threw it with disdain into the garden of the pub. He wasn't used to physical exertion but on this occasion he had no option. There were no roads leading to the little cottage, and even a bicycle wasn't a comfortable ride. He entered the premises under the sign bearing the legend "Fisherman's Rest" and a picture of a jolly old character in a heavy sweater and a pair of sea boots sitting next to a roaring fire, enticing thirsty customers to come in and spend their money. Slater was thirsty, but his primary concern was finding the people he was supposed to be meeting. He was already fifteen minutes late. Lenny would certainly suffer if he missed the appointment. He scanned the bar and then went into another part of the pub to where there were large cubicles each housing a table. This would be the sort of area his friends would choose to sit, somewhere that afforded a little bit of privacy, where conversations were seldom overheard. As he had anticipated, crowded around a table were four shadowy figures with empty glasses in front of them.

'Fitz, nice to see ya,' said Slater holding out his hand as if to welcome the visitor. The big man ignored the outstretched hand and instead peeled his left cuff away from his watch; he then gave Slater a quizzical stare.

'Yeh, I'm sorry, Fitz. I had to get here on a bike and Lenny was late and ...'

'Lenny?' interrupted Fitz. 'You haven't got that prat have you? No wonder you're late. If that's anything to go by, Slater, we may as well leave you to it now. We don't like being messed about.'

'Okay, okay,' replied Slater urgently. 'Things are cool I assure you. As I said to you before, Lenny is looking after our insurance at the moment. Nothing can go wrong; only one obstacle lies in our path, boys, and that is the location of the diamond. The police have already taken the house apart and didn't find anything. Still, they wanted to leave it as they found it, whereas we ...'

He left the rest unsaid. Slater left the group of men and went to the bar to fetch drinks for them all. The men at the table huddled closer together and had a brief discussion until Slater returned.

'What's the score then, Slater?' asked Fitz.

'It's quite simple gentlemen,' he began. 'We simply go to the house where the old man will be alone, apart from his little nephew. They'll give us no trouble, in fact when he finds out we've got his favourite neighbours, he will be only too happy to give us the diamond. He must know where it is. If his memory fails him, then he won't have many things left in his world. The first place to start is upstairs above the conservatory; he's got a sort of observation platform where he spends a lot of time. I take it you brought the right gear?'

'Don't insult us, Slater. Look, I don't particularly like you, and I'm only doing this out of respect for your father. This had better be a quick job and when do we get our cut?'

'Oh come on Fitz. Don't be naive. The stone needs to be treated first then sold. I don't double cross people. You'll get your whack, all of you, don't worry. Do you know where Jamaica Bay is?'

Fitz got to his feet downing what was left of his drink. 'Of course we do. We'll meet you on the main road outside.'

'You can't,' protested Slater. 'How am I going to get there? I'm on a bike. You must have room in your car.'

'I hate working with amateurs,' seethed Fitz. 'If brains were dynamite, I doubt you'd have enough to blow your nose.'

The other three men got up from the table, and for the first time Slater saw the size of them. He had requested that Fitz bought some 'animals' with him, and on that score he was certainly not disappointed. Despite the weather, all the men wore zip-up leather jackets and dark-coloured trousers like some sort of uniform. Their hair was very short, and Slater decided he would certainly not wish to meet any of these characters in a dark alley alone. They all left the pub and walked around the corner to the car park, where with great difficulty all five men squeezed into a moderately sized BMW. With the exhaust in great danger of dragging on the road the vehicle drove off towards Jamaica Bay.

Chapter 14

Jim had waited half an hour; he crept back to the window and once again peered through, where the scene had not changed. Lenny was fast asleep, and the two captives were in their original positions. He rose to his full height making Maureen aware of his presence; he put his thumbs up in a gesture asking if they were okay. She nodded her head vigorously; he then mimed using a knife and fork to eat and smacked his lips. He pointed at Lenny and then at the door. He was trying to get Maureen to wake Lenny up and get him to leave the room to prepare some food. This would give Jim enough time to get in through the window and untie the girls. It took him ten minutes to make himself understood, but eventually Maureen managed to wake their sleepy guard.

'Benny, Kenny,' she shouted. 'Lenny, whatever your name is, wake up.'

The snoring stopped, and Lenny sat bolt upright in his chair waving his gun from side to side.

'What's happened? Eh? What is it?' Realising everything was still under control he sank back and breathed a sigh of relief.

'Thank goodness for that. I thought Slater was back. He'd kill me if he had found me asleep. It's all right for him; I had to spend half the night and all morning squatting in bushes. What do you want anyway?'

'Isn't it about time we had some food? I'm absolutely starving,' lied Maureen.

'Didn't his lordship give you anything?'

'No, he didn't,' she replied.

'Actually, thinking about it, I could do with a sarnie or something,' said Lenny as he got to his feet and stretched his arms high in the air, submitting to an enormous yawn as he did so. Then tucking his gun into the waistband of his trousers he went over to Maureen and Gemma to check that they were still securely tied up. 'No, I don't think there is any danger of you not being here when I get back. We wouldn't want you to go walkies, would we?' he mocked.

Laughing to himself he opened the door and went through the dining room into the kitchen.

From where Jim was he could hear him whistling, very happy with himself and, no doubt, the prospect of being considerably richer in the near future. In one swift motion, the boy hauled himself up through the window and into the lounge.

'Jim!' exclaimed Maureen. 'How long have you known we were here?'

'Since yesterday,' Jim whispered. 'But there's no time to explain now.' He took the knife from his belt and cut

Maureen's bonds. Giving the knife to her, he ran to the door and quietly closed it. Then taking the length of twine from his pocket, he tied the door latch to the door latch housing. It was one of the old fashioned locks with a lever that lifted a bar into a keeper.

Gemma was now free. 'What are we going to do?' she asked.

'Do you remember the blocked off passage?' Not waiting for an answer he went on, 'Well believe it or not it comes out at the bottom of your well.' Maureen looked on in fascination.

'What on earth are you talking about, passages? What passages?'

Jim said, 'I'm sorry you'll just have to trust me. If we go to the well there are steps to climb down, we have to go now.'

He indicated the window and Gemma reacted first by easily climbing through into the garden.

At that moment Lenny came back and found he couldn't get into the room. 'Hey, what's going on, open this door. Open it now'

Maureen needed no further persuasion as she quickly followed her daughter.

'Open the door, or there'll be trouble!' yelled Lenny.

As Jim sat balanced, half in, half out of the room, a shot rang out, and splinters flew from the door. The bullet made a wet sounding splat as it buried itself in the old plaster above the fireplace. Realising that wouldn't work, Lenny started charging the door. Jim jumped down just in time to see Lenny fall into the room as the door disintegrated under his pressure. The boy ran to the well. Gemma and her mother were already descending the sheer walls of the hole.

'There are some torches at the bottom. Get going quickly,' he shouted. Lenny just saw the boy's head disappearing down the well. 'Kid, stop. I'll … I'll shoot,' he stammered. He saw his cut slipping out of his rather sticky grasp as the three escaped. A shot rang out but missed even the well, let alone endangering the life of anyone. Lenny had never fired a gun before today. He didn't really like them, but Slater insisted he should carry one. Seeing the confusion before him, Uncle Tom nearly broke cover to confront the man shooting at his nephew. It's as well he didn't though. He would never have got there. The man hidden behind him would have made sure of that.

Lenny came out of the house and ran to the well. 'Come back!' he shouted.

Almost sobbing at his failure he again pointed his gun, this time down the well. The shot rang out but by this time Jim had already started out down the passage. There was nothing left for Lenny except to pursue his quarry. Swinging his legs over the low wall, he felt for a foothold and lowered himself over the edge. He quickly got to the bottom and found the tunnel. This time he thought twice about firing his gun. The ricochets could be catastrophic; instead, he tried as quickly as possible to negotiate the low-ceilinged tunnel. By now Gemma and her mother had reached the other passage, Jim wasn't far behind them.

'I'm right behind you,' yelled Lenny. 'There's no escape, not from Lenny, and when I get you, you'll be sorry.'

There was only about twenty metres between them. It was here that Jim had his best idea. He had reached the junction of the tunnels. Fumbling in the large pouch on his belt he produced the safety flare his uncle had given him. Ripping away the paper guard around the fuse, Jim pointed it towards the well and pulled violently.

At first nothing happened, but then the flare exploded with a fizz and a brilliant white light lit the passage down to where Lenny was cowering, shielding his eyes. Heat started to emanate from the small beacon as the boy carefully placed it on the floor. Remaining very calm he took the old wooden barrel top and did his best to wedge it back into position using the small wooden blocks. It wouldn't stop Lenny for very long but what he was counting on was the fact that Lenny didn't have a torch. Turning quickly left, he followed the tunnel down to the cave.

Meanwhile, as Lenny had disappeared down the well, Uncle Tom stood from his position and hurried off to get to his bridge, where he could see if the Cornish Pride had managed to reach the right spot. Behind him the silent stranger reached into his bag, produced a radio and spoke into it.

'The birds have flown but the crow is following.'
Replacing the radio he then disappeared back into the undergrowth.

After only twenty or thirty seconds Jim heard a smash of wood. Lenny was through. Not only that but Jim saw a faint glow behind him. The bungling criminal had actually done something right for a change. He had picked up the flare and was using it to light his way. The flares were designed to be held in the hand, which was something that Jim hadn't thought of.

When he got to the cave, Gemma and her mother were already in the dinghy with the oars ready. Jim climbed hurriedly down from the platform. With one hand still on the platform, Jim was untying the boat's mooring when Lenny burst into the cave.

'Well blimey,' he said looking round. 'You've really hit the jackpot here, haven't you?'

As Jim released the dinghy, he grabbed the iron bar he had left there the night before. Just as Lenny once again produced the gun, Jim lifted the bar and threw it with all his might. It hit Lenny on the shoulder sending him reeling backwards as his gun went off. The shot echoed right around the cave, making Gemma and her mother put their hands to their ears. As Lenny fell backwards he struck his head against the solid wall. For a moment he lay there, his gun gone, lost to the bottom of the flooded cavern floor. The dinghy by this time was at the mouth of the cave slipping gently under the overhang.

Lenny lurched to his feet, and with a despairing 'No, stop,' he dived into the water.

The fierce undercurrent plucked at his legs. Unfortunately for Jim, in all the excitement he had left the boat's painter trailing behind as he pulled hard on the oar.

Lenny managed to grab the floating line, holding on for grim death as the dinghy emerged from the cave. The sea almost boiled where the craggy rocks barred the way, making whirl-pool patterns all around the boat. These were the rocks that effectively hid the cave from the open sea. The channel between the sea and cliff was very narrow. As if speaking for the first time, Maureen let out all her emotions — realising that Lenny was still in tow, she screamed. 'AAAAHHHH!! Jim, that animal is still following us. Row faster, faster, he can't get us now, not now.'

Looking back, Jim saw Lenny struggling to stay afloat, trying to pull himself closer to the rubber craft. The eddying currents were tossing him about like a piece of driftwood. Maureen and Jim were still pulling hard on their oars but the currents made it very hard work.

'Jim, quick!' shouted Maureen, 'he's nearly caught us.'

Sure enough, Lenny was only a couple of metres from his target, pulling hand over hand narrowing the gap between them. Thinking swiftly, Jim whipped out the knife his Uncle had given him, and in the nick of time severed the line.

As he drifted away from the boat Lenny let out a maniacal scream. 'Slater will kill me ... Come back ... I can't swim ... please help me.'

Maureen, Gemma and Jim stopped rowing and laughed as, like a beached seal, Lenny clambered up onto some very uncomfortable-looking rocks. He was safe.

It was then that a loud siren vented across the sea. The occupants of the dinghy looked up to see the Cornish Pride doing its best to speed towards them. Maureen and Gemma were astonished to see them but what surprised Jim was the number of people on the boat and indeed, their identities. Not only were the crew in attendance but also several rather serious looking policemen including Bob Smith's brother, all of whom spontaneously burst into applause and whoops of support as they got closer and saw that everyone was okay.

'Has that chap still got a gun?' asked P.C. Smith across the churning water.

'I don't think so,' said Jim. 'I'm afraid he may have dropped it when I hit him with an iron brick.'

They all laughed. It wasn't long before all three were safely on board the fishing boat. Frank looked at Jim with that sparkle in his eye and gently slapped Jim on the shoulder. 'Well done, lad, very well done. You are brave.'

Jim smiled. He was proud, but all that mattered was that things would turn out for the best.

Lenny was still clutching the slimy weather-beaten cliff face, and looked almost relieved when Nobby threw him a lifeline, which he grasped thankfully. There was certainly no shortage of hands to drag the felon aboard. He was immediately wrapped in a blanket and given a nice pair of shiny handcuffs to wear.

'Have you got any idea how Uncle Tom's doing?' asked Jim.

'Oh I think he's being looked after,' said Bob. 'When I heard you talking to Frank yesterday I couldn't help telling my brother, so things are going to be all right. Don't worry.'

Uncle Tom had had a bit of a fright; he had hurried back towards Jamaica Bay after seeing Lenny give chase down the well. As he got to the house he felt a big hand on his shoulder pull him back. As the old man twisted round to see who it was, he suffered a murderous thump to his stomach. He fell to the ground, coughing and spluttering, the wind temporarily taken out of him. He looked up at the towering figure of Fitz who stood above him, sniffing.

'Oh dear old man, did we fall over? Let me help you up,' he said.

Slater appeared from behind him. 'Well well, I do believe we have some unfinished business to attend to. Shall we?' he said, gesturing to Uncle Tom to go into the house.

The old sailor stood his ground. 'What do you want Slater?'

'I want the diamond, old man. I've threatened you, I've warned you, I've even burnt your car. Well today you will either tell me where to find my inheritance or you will be left without a home. Oh and there's the little matter of your dear friend Maureen. Yes Maureen, I have her in my safe custody.'

'I don't think you do, Slater.' The voice came from the house. Slater looked around in astonishment.

'OK lads, out you come.' Sergeant Mineards gave the command, and at least fifteen uniformed police officers came out from the bushes and from behind the house. Some levelled powerful-looking weapons at the five men in leather jackets.

'Put down your weapons, Slater,' called the sergeant. 'My men will do whatever they think necessary to prevent harm to any member of the public, so don't be silly.'

Baseball bats, knives, knuckle dusters and an ancient looking pistol clattered to the dusty ground. Fitz took a couple of steps towards Slater and before anyone could stop him he drove a heavy gloved fist into his partner's face, sending him to the floor holding his face as blood laced through his fingers. Several policemen pulled the big man away from the figure writhing on the ground.

A large white van appeared down the dusty lane from the main road. It pulled up sharply and the five bewildered men were led away. They could look forward to a long stretch in prison.

Uncle Tom was, by this time, back on his feet, and very confused by the speed of the developments that had overtaken him.

'Are you okay, Tom?' asked Sergeant Mineards.

'Yes I think so, Colin. Thanks, but how on earth did you know what Slater was going to do?' mused Uncle Tom.

The old policeman chuckled, 'Oh it's a long story, but I've got a bone to pick with you as to why you chose to do this thing all on your own, with a young lad as well.'

There were many questions to ask and many more answers to be given, but all the old man could think about now was his nephew.

Seeing his concern the policeman said, 'Don't worry about Jim and the girls. They are safe and sound and on their way back to Pentilrock.'

Satisfied, Uncle Tom sat on his swinging chair under the veranda and sucked peacefully on the empty clay pipe that he produced from his pocket. Things hadn't turned out too bad.

The Final Chapter

The police had completed their search, removing anything that had been left in the cave. Maureen, Gemma and Jim had been brought back to Jamaica Bay by Frank, and they sat around the kitchen table with Uncle Tom and Sergeant Mineards. Everyone was holding separate conversations, all excitedly telling their own tale, because they all had their own special version. With Gemma and Maureen getting most of the attention, Jim made an excuse and went to the attic. Pinky looked very pleased to see his human friend as the young boy carried the wooden box down to the kitchen.

Upon his return, Frank was explaining, 'Once Tom and Jim had left yesterday, young Bob Smith came back from town with Colin, here.' The fisherman's big hands worked busily trying to demonstrate the tale being told.

'I told him all that I knew and suggested he sent a few of his lads with me, as a sort of reception committee in case they came after Jim and the girls.'

Everybody was silent as they heard the whole business unwind. Sergeant Mineards took up the story.

'Well you must understand the difficulty we were left in — with Maureen and little Gemma hostages, was it right to leave a young lad like Jim to do our dirty work? But the deciding factor as far as I was concerned was the secret tunnels. Nobody but Jim and Gemma knew them, which could be a major flaw in any plan we implemented. But I don't want you to think we just left the girls to it. As soon as we knew of the situation we had the cottage under constant observation. In fact Tom, as you sat in the bushes, you nearly used our man as a cushion, he was that close to you.'

'Well I'll be. In all my years of life on the high seas I don't think I've ever been so excited over goings on. But what I'm eager to find out is what happened to you girls? How did it happen? Did Slater hurt you?'

'No he didn't.' said Maureen. 'I feel quite sorry for him really. He is just a sad man trying to follow in his father's footsteps and live up to other people's expectations. He even had that idiot Lenny as a partner. He was very accident prone. He cut his finger making himself a sandwich. We were fine really. I was very proud of Gemma — she was very brave. They kept us tied up nearly all the time unless they were both there, which wasn't very often. I can't tell you the relief we felt when that little face appeared at the window. I never imagined though that Jim could have accomplished so much by himself. I'm so grateful.'

And so the scene was set for Jim to tell his side of the story. 'I'd never have found that tunnel from the cottage if Slater hadn't sat on the well whilst I was in it. I'd only gone there to see if you two were back from Exeter.'

He was now warming to his subject and he had everyone's attention as he sat hugging the pet mouse in his box.

'Me and Gemma found the tunnel by accident when we lost Pinky here, in the cellar. We had planned to have a good look round because by the look of things down there nobody had used the tunnel for a long time. We felt that if there was anything special to find it may be hidden there.'

'Well there's no need to bother now,' said Uncle Tom. 'Sergeant Mineards' men have done that and found nothing except what you left there.'

'We had all the things ready to go down and have a look round, so when we got that letter from Maureen I took the stuff to the cave myself. As I said, it was only luck that I found the passage from the well and managed to unblock it. I did find something else though Uncle Tom, but first will you have a look in here.'

He passed the wooden box to his great uncle and said, 'I'm a bit worried about Pinky. He's not moving around much, what do you think is wrong with him.'

The old man peered into the box. 'Well for a start you have got too much straw in here, the poor little thing, and what's this bag doing in here? Hang on.' The big hands pulled at the canvas bag with the holes around the top. 'What's this, Shrimp?' he asked. Everyone around the table leant forward to see what was in the small sack. The old sailor's expression changed as he pulled his hand from the bag, filling it was the transparent stone shining with pinks, greens and light blues lighting up the old man's face.

'The White Tiger!' said Uncle Tom. There was silence for a few seconds until the full realisation hit everybody. They all gathered round Jim, slapping him on the back and rubbing his head. He even got a big hug from Maureen. Everybody took it in turns to hold it gasping with joy and excitement.

'Where, may I ask, did you find it?' asked Sergeant Mineards when the laughing and chattering died down.

'It was in the cave, attached to a chain under the water. I hope I did right, only I thought it best to keep it a secret until everything had finished.'

'You did really well, you young scallywag,' said his great uncle. 'this calls for a celebration.' At that moment, Bob Smith's brother came in from the back yard. He was holding the iron brick Jim had floored Lenny with.

'This metal bar Jim, is this what you found under the water?' His eyes opened wide as he spied the diamond.

'Yes,' replied Jim. 'I found it with the diamond. I thought it was probably to weigh down the bag to stop it drifting away.'

'You had quite a find, didn't you?' said the policeman. 'I wouldn't have given it a second look but something caught my eye.'

He turned the block over in his hands and his face was illuminated by a golden glow which was reflected from the bright metal revealed partially under its steely coloured coat.

'Gold!' exclaimed Uncle Tom. 'It's gold.'

 'It certainly looks that way,' replied PC Smith, 'a lot of gold. I hate to think how much it is worth.'

They all sat down again, some breathing hard, others jabbering away at the person next to them, barely able to believe the events and outcomes of the last few days. Eventually, after a lot of excited talking and the consumption of gallons of tea and orange squash, Sergeant Mineards and his men left. They took the valuable items away for safe keeping, promising to return to Jamaica Bay the next day to tie up all the "loose ends". It was as well for Uncle Tom, Maureen, Jim and Gemma, the police did return. As soon as the news got out about the incredible adventure and the recovery of the The White Tiger, hordes of reporters, photographers and camera crews camped out at the front of the old wooden house. There was even a T.V. crew from Holland. Strange faces were seen trying to peer in at every window, trying to get a glimpse or a photo of the unlikely heroes.

For a few days, the four unfortunate subjects became household names throughout Britain. There wasn't a news programme or paper without their photographs being present or a quote from the many interviews that were given. Jim's mum, recovering from her operation in hospital, also got a lot of attention. In a way for Jim, that was the only sad bit. He couldn't tell his mum and dad all about it. The young hero was just pleased that his mum would be getting better soon.

On one of the many occasions that the phone rang, Jim was called to the phone, it was his mum and he got very emotional telling her all about it. He cried and she cried and even his dad came on and cried. His parents desperately wanted to come down and see him but his mum was still too weak.

For a few days after the arrest of Slater and his friends, Jim and Uncle Tom found that their time was not their own. Maureen and Gemma had the same problem. A steady stream of visitors arrived one after the other and sometimes all together. At one stage there were so many people milling about outside Jamaica Bay that an ice cream van arrived and did a thriving business. Jim and Gemma didn't mind that too much because the man inside the van, who wore a permanently huge smile, would not accept any money from the young celebrities for their ice cream cornets.

On the second afternoon following the discoveries, several police motorcycles arrived followed by a large black stretched limousine. The sightseers at the front of the house stepped back respectfully as the chauffeur elegantly got out of the wonderful shiny car and importantly held open the rear door for its occupant to get out. A fairly short but very smart man announced to the waiting crowd and Uncle Tom, Maureen, Gemma and Jim, that he was the representative of the Queen of Holland who had personally sent him along to thank all those involved for their endeavour and bravery. His name was Mr Van der Burg.

Uncle Tom invited him inside and Maureen set to making cups of tea, coffee and plates full of sandwiches. The important visitor, together with the crew of the Cornish Pride and Sgt Mineards, seemed to enjoy them immensely. When they had all eaten enough, Mr Van der Burg told them why he had been sent.

'Our whole country is very relieved and overjoyed at the recovery of the The White Tiger. We all thought we had lost it forever. In appreciation of the momentous act of its recovery, Her Majesty has instructed me to hand over this small token of our thanks to you all.'

Uncle Tom took the cheque from the smiling official and, as his mouth fell open in disbelief, the others gathered round to see the amount of money the cheque was written out for. It was more money than Jim could ever dream about having and he immediately looked at his uncle. Both of them knew now that the old sailor may well have enough money to buy Jamaica Bay for himself, with more than enough left over for Jim and his parents, as well as a bit for Maureen and Gemma.

That evening, after the girls had left for home, Jim and his uncle sat on the veranda of the old house enjoying the cool evening breeze, swinging gently on the comfortable chair. Maybe things would calm down a bit now and, perhaps Jim would have time to enjoy the rest of his holiday with his great uncle. The boy slipped his hand through the big man's arm and pulled himself closer.

'Well, what's up Shrimp?' Those ageing eyes sparkled deep blue as he looked down on his nephew.

Jim said in a quiet voice, 'I was just thinking, that's all. I told you didn't I?'

'You told me? Told me what lad?' The old man's tone was quizzical.

'I told you something would turn up!' A mischievous grin broke across Jim's little face and the two unmatched figures sat there together, laughing at each other, the sound of their pleasure drifting away into the still summer evening.

The author would like to thank the following people without whose help this book could not have been published

Glen, for all her encouragement and advice

Jo, for putting up with late nights and short tempers

Alison for her superb input and guidance

Colin Bradbury MBE for the cover illustration

All at plod publications for their friendly help and for the fact that they give new authors a chance.